Claire had timed her entrance to the Valentine Day's party to make sure that Aaron would have already arrived and been waiting for her—but not for too long. Surely he had to be there somewhere, she figured as she tried to part the sea of bodies on the stairway.

"Have you seen Aaron Mendel?" Claire asked a guy in a plaid flannel shirt.

"Who?" the guy asked, brushing against her as he leaned in to hear her better.

"Aaron Mendel. Have you seen him?" she repeated with all the patience she could muster.

"I think I saw him go up that way," the guy said, waving his beer toward a hallway to the right. "But that was a while ago."

"Thanks," Claire shouted as she made her way in the direction he had indicated. At least she was now certain that Aaron had arrived.

Claire turned the corner and, to her surprise, bumped into a very stunned-looking Zoey.

"What's the matter?" Claire asked her, directing her gaze into the room Zoey had just come from.

But she didn't need to wait for an answer. Right in front of her, Aaron was making out with some redhead.

MAKING OUT # 14

Aaron lets go

KATHERINE APPLEGATE

ON FLARE BOOK

AVON BOOKS, INC.
1350 Avenue of the Americas
New York, New York 10019

Copyright © 1996 by Daniel Weiss Associates, Inc., and Katherine Applegate
Published by arrangement with Daniel Weiss Associates, Inc.
Library of Congress Catalog Card Number: 98-93669
ISBN: 0-380-80870-6
www.avonbooks.com/chathamisland

First Avon Flare Printing: July 1999

AVON FLARE TRADEMARK REG. U.S. PAT. OFF. AND IN OTHER COUNTRIES, MARCA
REGISTRADA, HECHO EN U.S.A.

Printed in the U.S.A.

WCD   10   9   8   7   6   5   4   3   2   1

Aaron lets go

Claire was acutely aware of the stares she received as she entered the Valentine's Day party. If she hadn't already known she looked hot in her tight red velour shirt and black miniskirt, the appreciative looks from every guy in the room would have told her so. But Claire was accustomed to being admired. With long dark hair, Ivory-girl skin, smoldering eyes, and a body that made teenage guys lose their train of thought, she looked more like a supermodel than a senior in high school.

Claire let a pleased smile form on her lips. Being the best-looking girl in the house had its advantages, but none that she was planning to capitalize on that night. She had bigger fish to fry.

She scanned the living room in search of Aaron's dark brown hair and full red lips. But she couldn't find him. As Claire turned to leave the room she nearly caused Lucas to spill the extra glass of punch he had in his hand.

"Oops!" she said as they both started laughing. "You should learn not to sneak up on people like that, Cabral." She had to shout over the music.

"And you should learn not to make such sudden movements at crowded parties," he yelled back.

1

"If you're looking for Zoey," she said, leaning in so
that she didn't have to scream, "I didn't see her in
here."

"I know," he replied. "She went upstairs to find the
bathroom."

Claire nodded. Zoey was one of those girls who always headed for the bathroom. She was so predictable.

"You look great, Claire," Lucas said, giving her outfit an admiring glance. "Too bad you're wasting all that
on a creep like Aaron Mendel."

Claire didn't expect Lucas to understand her feelings
for her tall, dark, handsome, picture-perfect boyfriend.
After all, thanks to Claire, Lucas had walked in on
Aaron making out with Zoey. "Stop pouting, Lucas,"
she said in his ear. "You've already had your chance."

She pulled back to see Lucas's grinning face. He
might be on the simple side, Claire thought, but she had
to admit that Lucas could always appreciate a good
line. She waved good-bye and took off to find Aaron.

There had been a time when she'd thought seriously
about Lucas. He had been her first boyfriend, maybe
even her first love. And he had spent two years in Youth
Authority taking the rap for a crime she'd committed,
which was kind of romantic when you thought about it.
Claire even had the sense that she could take Lucas
away from Zoey if she wanted to. But she didn't want
to. Why would she, when she had Aaron? Unlike Lucas,
he was her equal in every way. If only she could find
him, Claire would show Aaron just how much he meant
to her. But where was he? Claire had timed her entrance to make sure that Aaron would have already arrived and been waiting for her—but not for too long.
Surely he had to be there somewhere, she figured as she
tried to part the sea of bodies on the stairway.

"Have you seen Aaron Mendel?" Claire asked a guy

2

in a plaid flannel shirt who had been eyeing her breasts.

"Who?" the guy asked, brushing against her as he leaned in to hear her better.

"Aaron Mendel. Have you seen him?" she repeated with all the patience she could muster.

"I think I saw him go up that way," the guy said, waving his beer toward a hallway to the right. "But that was a while ago."

"Thanks," Claire shouted as she made her way in the direction he had indicated. At least she was now certain that Aaron had arrived.

Claire turned the corner and, to her surprise, bumped right into a very stunned-looking Zoey.

"What's the matter?" Claire asked her, directing her gaze into the room Zoey had just come from.

But she didn't need to wait for an answer. Right in front of her, Aaron was making out with some redhead.

One

Claire Geiger slowly became aware that her fingernails were digging into the soft skin of her palms. The sharp pain brought her vision back into focus. She'd thought for a second that she was hallucinating.

The possibility that Aaron Mendel, the love of her life, was at that moment passionately kissing a girl other than herself had seemed out of the question. But Claire's eyesight was 20/20. And she was looking straight at her boyfriend. And he was sticking his tongue so far down another girl's throat that he was probably able to taste what she'd had for dinner. So much for Valentine's Day.

Out of the corner of her eye, Claire saw Zoey Passmore and Lucas Cabral exchanging worried glances. "Claire?" Zoey said.

"Don't talk to me," Claire answered softly. "No one talk to me."

"Claire, please—" The pity in Zoey's wide blue eyes made bile rise in Claire's throat. Or was it the fact that she'd been fool enough to pine away for a no-good, two-timing sleaze-bag that was making her gag?

When she felt Zoey's hand close around her upper arm, Claire twisted from her friend's grasp. "I mean it, Zoey. Keep your mouth shut."

Claire stared at the girl in Aaron's arms for one more second, allowing the sight to imprint itself on her brain. Because the girl's back was to her, Claire couldn't see much but her long red hair. Her fingers ached to pull out one of the tramp's springy curls, but Claire forced herself to remain calm.

She turned away from the gruesome sight. She wouldn't talk to him. There would be no shouting or crying or lame excuses. Claire wasn't about to degrade herself further by creating a pathetic scene for the amusement of a bunch of boarding-school geeks.

She felt the muscles in her neck and back tighten as she walked sedately down the hallway. The stairs seemed to wobble under her feet as she descended to the first floor, and for a moment she thought she would faint. But Claire kept her gaze fixed on the front door, silently counting down the seconds until she would reach the exit and make her escape.

Outside, a cold drizzle had started to fall. Claire breathed in the damp air, filling her lungs with oxygen. Although her first instinct was to collapse on the grass and sob herself into oblivion, she resisted. She knew Zoey would be trotting after her any second now, and she wanted to avoid sympathetic pats on the back at all costs.

Claire headed in the direction of the Mercedes she'd parked down the street earlier. Had that been only ten minutes before? She felt as though a year had passed since she'd pulled the key out of the ignition and checked her lipstick one final time in the rearview mirror.

Don't think, Claire told herself. *Just get out of here.* She continued toward the car, clutching her sleek leather jacket to her chest like a security blanket. Drops of rain created large stains on her blouse, and the heels of her platform shoes were collecting bits of wet grass and mud. But Claire didn't notice—or care.

She just wanted to get in the Mercedes and go somewhere. She needed to be away from Aaron and his beautifully shaped mouth. Away from Zoey's worried face and Lucas's uncomfortable grimaces. Unfortunately, Claire knew, even her iron will wouldn't save her from her own tortured thoughts. The sting of humiliation and heartbreak, she realized, sucked the big one.

Jake McRoyan stared at the rain falling outside the front window of Ernie's Grill. From where he stood, the nearly empty streets of Weymouth looked almost eerie. He ran a hand through his short dark hair, wondering how he'd gotten to this bizarre point in his life.

A few weeks earlier, Jake would have thought a cold, wet night was a perfect backdrop for getting a couple of six-packs or a bottle of vodka and drinking until he passed out on the floor of his bedroom. Despite the fact that he was fanatical about his place on the football team in the fall and the basketball team in the winter, he'd been willing to punish his body on an almost daily basis.

Sometimes a few weeks could constitute a lifetime.

"I'm ready," a soft voice said in his ear.

"Great." Jake turned to look at Louise Kronenberger. Tall, blond, and busty, Louise was the kind of girl that guys like Jake spent years joking about in the locker room after football practice. The K-Burger had been the "first" for more than a handful of guys in Weymouth High's senior class. Including Jake. He'd lost his virginity to Louise in a drunken stupor at a homecoming party the previous fall. Now it was winter, and they were attending Alcoholics Anonymous meetings to-

6

gether. Life was funny like that. Not funny ha-ha. But funny weird.

Jake opened the door and waited while Louise struggled to get her umbrella open. "I'll walk you to the water taxi," she offered.

Along with the rest of the kids he'd grown up with, Jake lived on Chatham Island, which was about four miles off the coast of Maine. Since he'd already missed the last ferry, he'd have to shell out forty bucks for a water taxi.

"Thanks," he said, taking hold of the umbrella and positioning it over both their heads.

As they walked down the street Jake was silent. He still hadn't figured out whether going out for a Valentine's Day dinner with Louise after their AA meeting had been a friendly let's-support-each-other thing or a more serious this-is-our-first-date thing. Furthermore, he wasn't sure what he *wanted* the night to be. Who would've thought that he'd ever be totally sober, walking in the rain with the K-Berger, trying to decide whether or not he should make a move?

Finally Louise gave him a half smile. "What're you thinking?" she asked. Even when she was sober, her voice was deep and husky.

Jake shrugged. "About how fast things change sometimes."

"Yeah," Louise agreed. "At this time last year I was so drunk I didn't notice that Tim Crawley's waterbed had sprung a leak until his mom walked in and found us half naked. We were twisted up in a tangle of wet sheets and empty beer cans."

"Sounds, uh, interesting," Jake said. He felt a blush rising to his cheeks at the thought of Louise naked. "Last Valentine's Day I was with Zoey. . . ."

"Oh, yeah. Sweet, perfect Zoey. The angel who

dropped you like a bad habit the minute Lucas got back to town."

Jake pressed his lips tightly together. *Be cool*, he cautioned himself. Even though he and Zoey had broken up months before, Jake still felt very protective toward her. The sad fact was that Zoey was probably the best friend Jake had just then. "You have a problem with Zoey?" he asked.

Louise shook her head. "Forget I said anything."

"Fine. I will."

Neither spoke again until they reached the pier where the water taxi was docked. Jake stopped in front of the wooden dock and handed Louise her umbrella. His heart had started beating quickly, and he felt slightly short of breath. He had about twenty seconds to answer the ten-million-dollar question: Should he kiss her? If so, should the kiss be a light peck on the lips? A warm kiss on the cheek? Would his tongue be involved?

Jake rubbed his palms together. He wasn't sure whether they were damp from rain, sweat, or both.

He cleared his throat. "Tonight was . . ."

"Weird?" Louise asked.

Jake laughed. Louise had a way of cutting through the bull. "Yeah, weird. But nice, too."

"Listen, Jake . . ." Her voice trailed off, and she suddenly seemed to find the handle of the umbrella a fascinating object of study.

Jake stared at Louise's soft lips. He wanted to kiss her. There was no doubt about it. He'd wanted to kiss her since dessert, when she'd had a small dab of whipped cream at the corner of her mouth. So he'd just do it. After all, they'd done a lot more than swap a little saliva in the past. This was nothing.

Jake took a step closer and put his hand softly on Louise's shoulder. With his left index finger he tilted her chin so that she was gazing into his eyes. Slowly he brought his lips within an inch of hers.

"Jake, wait," Louise said suddenly.

"What?" Jake instantly stepped back.

"This isn't a good idea."

"It's not?" Now that he'd mentally prepared himself to kiss Louise, his body was telling him that not only was physical contact a good idea, it was necessary.

"I . . . uh, sort of talked to my sponsor about you today," she said softly.

"Really?" Jake's voice wasn't much more than a squeak.

Most of the people in AA had a sponsor—a particular person whom they could talk to anytime, about anything. A sponsor was sort of a helper along the path of sobriety.

"Yeah. And she pretty much reiterated what I already knew."

"What's that?"

"Now isn't a good time for me to get involved. I've been sober for almost ninety days . . . and I don't want to do anything that's going to make me risk blowing it."

"And kissing me is a risk?"

Louise nodded. "Yep. For all kinds of reasons."

"Okay, then." Jake stepped back, leaving the shelter of the umbrella.

"See you at the meeting tomorrow," Louise said.

Jake waved. "Yeah. See ya."

He headed toward the water taxi, already dissecting his "date" with Louise.

While part of Jake still wished he'd kissed those soft lips, another part of him breathed a huge sigh of relief. For one thing, he still had to deal with Lara McAvoy and the fallout from the bizarre valentine she'd sent

9

him. He also knew from his AA meetings that getting involved with anyone, much less another alcoholic (sober or not), was a bad idea for at least his first year of teetotalism.

Then there was Louise herself. Sure, she'd been a great friend since he'd kicked his habit. And yes, she was sexy. But she was also Louise Kronenberger, class slut.

If he was completely honest with himself, Jake had to admit that dating a girl who had a reputation with a capital *R* could mean trouble. And he already had enough trouble to last a lifetime.

"Excuse me," Zoey said for the third time. She pushed past a guy who looked as though he'd stepped off the pages of the *Preppy Handbook* and reached for the doorknob.

Zoey had stood dumb in the hallway for almost a minute after Claire had left. She'd been torn between giving Kate Levin and Aaron Mendel a verbal bashing they'd never forget and racing after Claire, who seemed on the verge of an implosion. Finally Zoey had opted for Claire.

Zoey sprinted outside and scanned for Claire. She didn't see her. But halfway down the block she spotted the Geigers' Mercedes parked under a streetlamp. As Zoey jogged toward the car she tried to think of something comforting to say to Claire. Nothing came to mind.

When Zoey approached the driver's side of the car, she saw that Claire was inside, already strapped into her seat belt.

"Claire, roll down the window!" Zoey shouted.

Claire didn't respond. "Come on," Zoey yelled.

A moment later Lucas came up behind Zoey and

knocked on the car window. His longish blond hair was already damp from the rain, and Zoey could see the concern in his dark eyes. Zoey pushed her shoulder-length dark blond hair out of her face and hoped that Lucas would have more success at getting through to Claire than she'd had.

But Claire just shook her head and revved the engine. Then she turned away from Zoey and Lucas, staring into the dark night.

"You can't drive in this condition!" Lucas shouted.

"He's right," Zoey agreed, knocking on the window again.

Claire didn't seem to hear either of them. She shifted the car into drive.

"She's outta here," Lucas said. He guided Zoey gently to the curb. "Watch your toes."

A second later Claire pulled away from the curb and sped down the street. Zoey watched as the taillights of the Mercedes disappeared around the corner.

"Poor Claire," Zoey whispered.

Lucas nodded. "Well, this pretty much cements my opinion of Aaron. The guy is a sleaze."

Lucas didn't usually hold grudges, but Zoey knew he hated Aaron Mendel. Not that she blamed him. Before Claire and Aaron had started going out, Zoey had been involved with Aaron for what she regarded now as the stupidest few weeks of her life. She'd fooled around with Aaron a couple of months earlier, when he'd come to visit his mother on Chatham Island. Lucas had found it in his heart to forgive Zoey for cheating, but he still thought Aaron was pure slime.

Zoey's opinion of Aaron wasn't much higher than her boyfriend's, but she knew from experience that it took two to cheat. Aaron was one. Kate Levin was two.

"Don't forget your good friend Kate," Zoey

11

snapped. "She was practically glued to Aaron's chest."

"You really have it in for her, don't you?" Lucas said. "Jeez, Zo. She probably doesn't even know Aaron has a girlfriend."

Zoey rolled her eyes. Since Kate Levin, the daughter of Mrs. Cabral's childhood friend, had moved into the Cabrals' house, Zoey had been sure the girl was after Lucas. He kept insisting he and Kate had a brother-sister relationship, but Zoey thought Kate was being just a little too friendly.

"Lucas, I really don't feel like standing around in the freezing rain discussing Kate or Aaron. Let's just get out of here."

She headed toward the Passmores' van, which was parked across the street. So much for a night of slow dancing and making out in the corner. Valentine's Day had been an unmitigated failure.

Lucas caught her arm. "We just drove an hour and a half to get here."

"So?" Zoey raised her eyebrows.

"So maybe we should go back inside and try to salvage the evening."

Zoey pulled the car keys from her pocket. "Suit yourself. But I'm leaving." She stared at Lucas until he finally shifted his eyes toward the ground.

"I'll go get Kate," he muttered.

Inwardly Zoey groaned. She'd momentarily forgotten that Lucas had promised they'd give Kate a ride back to Weymouth. *Oh, well*, she thought. As long as Kate was in Zoey's line of vision, she could be sure the girl wasn't hooking her claws into Lucas or Aaron or some other hormonally challenged guy.

"Good idea," she said. "And grab my coat."

Two

Aaron Mendel stared at Kate Levin's full lips. What had he done? He'd come to this lame party to see Claire for the first time in weeks, and he'd just spent the last five minutes engaging in a serious PDA with an old summer fling. *Real bright, Mendel.*

Aaron quickly put several feet between himself and Kate. "This can't happen," he said.

Kate smiled, swaying toward him. "Why not?"

"Because I've got a girlfriend, and she's going to arrive here any minute."

Aaron's heart thudded in his chest. He wasn't used to caring about someone. In the past, he'd gotten whatever pleasure he could from the prettiest girl in a mile radius, then moved on without a second thought. But Claire had changed him. He loved her. Which meant he shouldn't be kissing another girl—even if she was gorgeous. And willing.

"I don't remember you being such an altar boy, Aaron," Kate said. She arched an eyebrow and stared into his eyes.

He shrugged, shifting his eyes from her gaze. "Times change."

"She's a lucky girl."

Aaron nodded. He definitely agreed with Kate on that

13

. Claire was lucky to have him. Hadn't he just
sed up an opportunity to make out with a sexy girl
cause he was so devoted to her? Okay, he'd allowed
imself to indulge in a little bit of making out. But he'd
stopped as soon as he realized his mistake.

Aaron took another step backward. He'd better give
Kate the brush-off immediately. Claire was sharp. If she
walked into the party and saw him even *talking* to Kate,
she might guess something wasn't kosher.

"Well, it was nice to see you—" Aaron began. He
stopped when he saw Lucas Cabral striding toward him.

"Hey, Cabral," Aaron said. He crossed his arms in
front of his chest and put on his most arrogant face.

But Lucas didn't even look at him. "Kate, we're
leaving," Lucas said.

"Why?" Kate asked. "You guys just got here."

Aaron felt a strange tightening in his chest. If Lucas
knew Kate, it was quite possible that Claire knew her,
too. This cozy conversation was verging on a delicate
situation.

"Zoey wants to leave," Lucas said to Kate. He still
hadn't looked directly at Aaron.

Aaron cleared his throat loudly. Being ignored made
him nervous. "You guys . . . know each other?"

"Yep," Lucas said shortly.

"Well, hey, what a coincidence," Aaron said, trying
to sound innocent. "Kate and I are old friends. We were
just, uh, catching up on old times."

Lucas snorted. "You can cut the crap, Aaron. Claire
saw the whole thing."

"What's going on here?" Kate asked. She looked
from Lucas to Aaron.

Lucas grimaced. "In case he forgot to mention it,
Aaron has a girlfriend. She lives on the island."

"And she saw us. . . ." Kate's voice trailed off.

"You got it," Lucas said coldly.

"Where's Claire now?" Aaron asked. Normally he prided himself on remaining cool and collected at all times, but he'd been caught off guard. He felt his composure slipping away as he regarded Lucas's cold, tight smile.

"She split," Lucas responded. "Zoey and I are going, too." He glanced back at Kate. "And so is Kate."

"Who said I was leaving?" Kate asked, turning to Lucas.

Aaron was gratified to see a slight blush rise to Lucas's cheeks. "I just assumed. . . ."

Kate laughed. "Suit yourself. But I plan to enjoy myself."

Despite his misery over the fact that Claire had seen him with another girl, Aaron was thoroughly enjoying Lucas's discomfort.

"How are you going to get home?" Lucas asked, his voice rising.

"I'm a big girl, Lucas. I think I can find my way from Portland to Weymouth." Kate took a step closer to Aaron.

Lucas turned to Aaron. "Do you have anything to say about this?"

Aaron gave Lucas what he knew was his most infuriating grin. "Last time I checked, it was a free country, Cabral. She can do whatever she wants."

Aaron watched as Lucas's face turned bright red. This moment was getting better and better. "I can't believe you're standing there like such a self-satisfied jerk," Lucas snarled. Aaron noticed little bits of spit flying from Lucas's mouth. "You should be off begging Claire's forgiveness. Not that I expect her to give you the time of day after this."

Kate stepped between Lucas and Aaron. "Call it

15

women's intuition, but I'm getting the feeling you guys don't like each other."

"You could say that," Lucas said.

"It's a long, boring story, Kate," Aaron said. "I'm sure Lucas would relish telling you every tedious detail, but he's on his way out."

Lucas glared at Aaron one last time, then turned his back. "I'll see you at home, Kate," he said over his shoulder.

As he watched Lucas's back retreat toward the door, the adrenaline that had been pumping through Aaron's veins slowed to a dull throb. Now that his confrontation with Lucas Cabral was over, he had to face reality. He was in deep, deep trouble with Claire Geiger. At this point he needed to focus on damage control. It was going to take a significant amount of brainpower to come up with a lie that would be good enough to explain away the kiss with Kate.

His thoughts were interrupted when he felt Kate's arms encircle his waist. "We're all alone now," Kate whispered. "Remember what we did last summer when we were alone?"

Aaron's hands involuntarily moved to Kate's shoulders. Man, did he remember. Images of Kate's naked body flashed before his eyes. He'd never considered her more than a casual fling, but she'd filled that role to perfection. Unlike Claire, Kate had been ready and willing to sleep with him.

"Let's get out of here," Aaron said softly.

Kate smiled. "I thought you'd never ask."

Aaron slipped his arm around Kate's shoulders and guided her toward the stairs. *Tomorrow I'll find a way to get Claire back. As for tonight . . . well, a little action never hurt anybody.*

* * *

Nina Geiger opened her gray eyes slowly when heard a bang, followed by a soft curse and the sou. of someone shuffling up a flight of stairs. For sever seconds Nina thought she was in her own bed, listening to Claire sneak into the house.

Then the memory of the night came rushing back. She'd hoped to have a romantic evening with Benjamin. But as had been the case every night with Benjamin since his surgery, events hadn't gone as planned.

Benjamin's mood had gone from bad to horrific after Nina had arrived at the Passmores'. When she'd tried to cheer him up, he'd become Hurricane Benjamin and destroyed half his bedroom. Finally he'd kicked Nina unceremoniously out of his room. She'd retreated to Zoey's bedroom and cried herself to sleep. Now she was a dead lump of slightly overweight (she'd never believe she had a good figure, no matter what Zoey kept insisting) flesh and tangled dull brown hair. Since the temporary red dye she had used in a fit of despair over Benjamin had washed out, her hair had not looked quite right.

The door of Zoey's bedroom opened, and Nina shifted her body so that she was leaning against Zoey's wall of pillows.

"Hi, honey, I'm home," she called.

Zoey jumped. "Nina?" she shrieked. "What are you doing here?"

"Hiding. And I'm not Nina. Nina was a girl who had an awesome boyfriend. I'm just a pale clone of the girl your brother once loved."

Even in the dim light, Nina could see Zoey shaking her head with exasperation. "You're Nina Geiger, queen of melodrama."

"If I'm the queen, Benjamin's the king."

Zoey switched on the small lamp that stood on her

side table. "I may not be psychic, but I'm getting vibe that you guys didn't have such a great time night."

That was the understatement of the year. Nina's evening had resembled a movie about the aftermath of a nuclear war.

"Hey, I really get a kick out of watching the guy I love tear posters off his wall, break his CDs, trash his furniture, and make mincemeat out of his Ray-Bans."

Zoey gasped. "Benjamin actually did all that?"

Nina nodded sadly. "And more."

Zoey sighed and sat down on the edge of the bed. "Wow."

"He's lost, Zo," Nina whispered. "He's off in his private, dark world."

"He's just confused," Zoey answered, getting up again and crossing the room toward her bureau. "He'll snap out of it. Eventually."

"Yeah?" Nina asked.

"Yeah." Zoey almost sounded convinced of it herself. Almost, but not enough to keep Nina's stomach from tightening into a painful ball.

Nina rolled onto her stomach and hid her face against a pillow. "Sometimes I wish Benjamin had never heard about that stupid operation. He never minded being blind before."

"Nina, he's always hated being blind," Zoey said in her most reasonable voice. "But before he found out about the experimental laser surgery that might have given him back his sight, he never allowed himself to admit it." She pulled out of the bottom drawer of her dresser the maroon Boston Bruins shirt she wore to bed every night.

"I guess he's dealing with it all over again, huh?" Nina asked. She sat up and reached for her backpack.

18

A conversation this depressing called for a Lucky Strike.

Zoey's head was hidden behind the Bruins shirt she was pulling on, but Nina could see that her best friend was nodding.

"You've got to be patient," Zoey said when her face emerged from the nightshirt.

Nina located a half-empty pack of cigarettes and popped a semicrushed Lucky Strike into her mouth. As usual, she puffed on the cigarette without lighting it. "Maybe I should go downstairs and try to talk to him again. He might be more mellow, if I catch him while he's unconscious."

"Uh, I don't know if that's such a good idea," Zoey said, putting her hair back in a red scrunchie that had seen better days.

"I thought you said he loves me." Nina took another long drag on the Lucky Strike.

"He *does*. But maybe not, like, at this moment. I mean, he doesn't love anyone right now."

Nina felt like crushing her cigarette into a million tiny bits of tobacco. She wanted Zoey to tell her that everything was fine and that of course Benjamin would be thrilled to wake up and find Nina in his bed. But no, Zoey had to be honest and objective.

"Man, just when life gets halfway bearable, reality sets in," Nina observed.

For years Nina had walked around in a haze of cynicism and bad moods. When she'd started going out with Benjamin, the clouds had parted and she'd been . . . happy. Okay, deliriously, sickeningly ecstatic. And she'd been stupid enough to believe she would stay that way.

Zoey flopped down next to Nina on the bed. "Tell me about it."

"Don't tell me your Valentine's Day wasn't all hearts and kisses," Nina observed.

"Hardly."

Nina felt herself perk up. "What happened?"

"Kate Levin happened." Zoey's voice was cold and angry.

Nina allowed herself to forget her own pain. She had a feeling she'd stumbled onto a major piece of island gossip. "You mean she, like, jumped Lucas's bones at the party?"

Zoey shook her head, looking irritated. "She jumped Aaron's bones. And Aaron jumped back."

Nina whistled softly. "Does Claire know?"

"She saw the whole thing."

"Man." Nina sighed. "I may be getting senile in my old age, but I actually feel sorry for the girl."

She flicked imaginary ash onto Zoey's bedspread and tried to imagine the look on Claire's face when she discovered her one true love examining another girl's tonsils with his tongue.

"It was pretty horrible," Zoey said. "I hope she's okay."

"Come on, Zo. Vampire Girl will find another poor sap to feed on, and she'll be fine in no time."

Zoey rolled her eyes. "Believe it or not, your older sister has feelings, Nina. I think I saw a tear in her eye."

Nina was speechless. She'd seen Claire annoyed. She'd seen her scheming. She'd even seen her so angry that the little vein next to her right eye started to pulsate. But she hadn't seen her sister cry since their mother died over five years before.

"Are you sure she was crying?" Nina asked. "I mean, maybe she'd been walking in the wind or something."

"She was crying," Zoey confirmed.

"So do you think she's home by now?"

"I don't know," Zoey said, yawning. "She was pretty ambiguous about her plans before we left for Portland. And after she saw Aaron and Kate, she just took off without a word."

Nina nodded to herself. "I think she was planning to stay in Portland for the night—with Aaron."

"Well, that's definitely not happening," Zoey commented.

Nina was suddenly exhausted. She felt as if she and everyone she knew was going through an emotional meat grinder. Being systematically turned to ground beef had drained her of all energy. Her eyelids were heavy, and the idea of walking across North Harbor to her house seemed like mission impossible.

"Can I stay here tonight?" she asked.

"Sure. But no smoking in bed." Zoey slipped under her thick comforter and closed her eyes.

Nina tossed her Lucky Strike into the trash can next to Zoey's bed and reached up to turn out the light. Zoey wasn't exactly the Passmore that Nina was dying to spend the night with, but beggars couldn't be choosers.

Nina stared into the darkness for a few moments, thinking of Benjamin, who was only a staircase and a short hall away. Then she closed her eyes, resigned to the fact that she was stuck with Zoey for the rest of the night. Benjamin might have been close in the geographical sense, but mentally he was on the other side of the planet.

"I wish I were dead," Nina said aloud.

Zoey grabbed the pillow from under her head and used it to smack Nina in the face. "Don't say that."

"Okay, I wish I were in a coma."

"As Scarlett O'Hara says at the end of *Gone with the Wind*, 'Tomorrow is another day.' "

"Frankly, my dear, I don't give a damn."

"Good night, Nina," Zoey said firmly.

" 'Night, Zo."

Nina rolled over onto her side. She tried to focus all her energy on thinking of a way to win back Benjamin's affection. But as she drifted into sleep all she felt was an overwhelming sense of hopelessness.

Three

Claire rolled over on the king-sized bed in her deluxe room at the Ritz-Carlton. Despite fluffy pillows and crisp white sheets, Claire had slept for a total of forty-five minutes. She'd spent the entire night going over every second of her relationship with Aaron Mendel.

The previous night was supposed to have been one of the best of her life. After closely guarding her virginity for almost eighteen years, she'd been ready to make the big leap into womanhood with the guy she was in love with. She'd even gone to the trouble of conning her dad into letting her rent a hotel room, courtesy of his Gold Card.

Of course, Burke Geiger was in such a dream world these days that he probably wouldn't have noticed if Claire had gone to Hawaii for a week. And the reason he was walking around on cloud nine was none other than Sarah Mendel, Aaron's mother.

Claire almost laughed at the irony. Her father had fallen in love with Sarah a few months before, which had led to Claire's falling in love with Aaron when he'd come to Chatham Island for the holidays. At the time, she'd thought the arrangement was perfect. As long as Mr. Geiger was involved with Mrs. Mendel, Claire could be assured that she'd get to see Aaron whenever he had time off from boarding school.

But Claire's good luck had evolved into a curse. If the couple went through with the marriage plans they'd announced on New Year's Eve, Aaron Scumdel would become her stepbrother. What a joke. Every time she saw her dad mooning over Sarah, she'd have to be reminded of the louse the woman called a son. He would haunt her.

Claire sat up in bed and rubbed her swollen eyes. There was no point in lingering there. She might as well head back to Chatham and her lonely, pathetic, extremely bitter life. As she swung her legs over the side of the bed, Claire heard a loud banging on the door.

Her heart jumped, and she raced across the room. Aaron had found her. He'd probably been up the whole night, trying to think of a way to beg her forgiveness. Despite herself, Claire smiled. She took a deep breath and swung the door open. "Don't even think I'm going to forgive—"

"Expecting someone else?" On the other side of the door was a woman with curly brown hair and round blue eyes. She was standing next to a large cart, which was stacked high with towels and small baskets of miniature soaps and shampoos.

She should have guessed. The maid. Claire stepped back to let the woman in. "No, I've been holding a grudge against you ever since I realized I was short one bath towel."

"Maybe I should come back later."

Claire shook her head. "No, now's fine. I'm leaving, anyway."

The woman stepped inside the room, then pulled the cart in behind her. "I'm Rosie."

Claire sank into an armchair, feeling even more desolate than she had a few moments before. "I'm Claire."

"You don't look so good, Claire."

"Yeah? Well, I feel like crap."

Rosie laughed, which was Claire's first reminder that while her world had come to a screeching halt, everyone else's was spinning as usual.

"Do you have a boyfriend?" Claire asked. Although she usually avoided idle chitchat with strangers, Claire sensed that Rosie could offer sympathy she'd never seek from her sister. Or, God forbid, her father.

"A husband," Rosie answered. She moved toward the bed.

Claire stood up to help Rosie strip the sheets. "Yeah?"

"Yep. Six years."

"Has he ever cheated on you?" Claire yanked off a pillowcase and wadded it into a ball.

"Are you kidding?" Rosie asked. "I'd kick his butt out the door so fast he wouldn't have time to put on his shoes."

Claire sighed, dropping the pillowcase at her side. "Men suck."

"Have a bad night?" Rosie asked. She took fresh linens from the cart and began remaking the bed.

"Somewhere in between getting a knife in the back and a stake in the heart." Claire sat back down in the armchair. She couldn't believe she was spilling her guts to the maid at the Ritz-Carlton. Or to anyone, for that matter.

"He must be pretty stupid to mess up something good with a girl like you."

Claire nodded. "I couldn't agree more."

For a few seconds Claire stared vacantly into space, mentally listing the various forms of torture she'd like to inflict upon the most sensitive areas of Aaron's body.

She finally settled on a scenario involving red ants and a jar of honey.

Feeling a little better, Claire reached into the leather overnight bag she'd brought and pulled out her new Victoria's Secret lace nightie. She could barely bring herself to touch it, much less wear the vile thing.

"Do you want this?" Claire asked Rosie, dangling the nightgown in front of her.

"Sure." Rosie deftly caught the tiny garment when Claire tossed it in her direction.

"Knock yourself out," Claire said.

"Well, thanks. Sam won't know what hit him."

Claire shrugged. "Hey, it was either give it to you or waste valuable time shredding it with my bare hands."

Rosie set the nightie on top of her cart and walked over to Claire. "Don't take it so hard, hon," she said, patting Claire gently on the back. "You're a sweet girl—and beautiful. You'll meet the right guy eventually."

Claire felt a fresh round of tears trying to fight their way out of her eyes. She'd been described in many ways: icy, snobby, intelligent, perfect. But never sweet.

At least she hadn't been called that in a long, long time. Who could have known that a thirtyish maid in a four-star hotel would be the closest thing to a mother that Claire would find in five years.

This is not happening, Aisha Gray said to herself. It was Saturday morning, and she'd stumbled out of her first-floor bedroom in search of caffeine.

But the scene taking place in the kitchen of her family's bed-and-breakfast had to be a continuation of the dream she'd just had about the Westinghouse scholarship exam. She'd thought the nightmare had ended with her dramatically stabbing David Barnes in the heart with a well-sharpened number-two pencil. Apparently she'd only *thought* she'd woken up.

Because it wasn't possible that her nemesis was sitting at the kitchen table, sipping coffee and eating pancakes. Aisha pinched herself. No luck—this was not a bad dream. And the fact that she hadn't bothered to run a comb through her curly black hair didn't make her feel any better. She wouldn't even think about the fresh zit she'd noticed on her usually smooth dark skin. She didn't care what she looked like in front of David. Not at all.

"Hi, Eesh," Mrs. Gray said in an annoyingly cheerful voice. She was standing in front of the stove's built-in griddle, pouring batter into perfect circles.

Aisha glared at her mother. "What's *he* doing here?"

Mrs. Gray raised her eyebrows. "Good morning to you, too."

"Nice to see you, Aisha," David said.

Mrs. Gray set down her ladle and picked up a spatula. "I gather you two know each other."

Aisha rolled her eyes. "We've met."

Until a few weeks before, David Barnes had been just a somewhat cute white guy who'd shown up in several of her advanced-placement classes. Okay, a very cute white guy.

Now he was her personal sadist. A couple of weeks earlier, Aisha had been informed that she was a finalist in the Westinghouse competition for academic merit. If she won the competition—which evaluated her overall academic excellence in science and included a grueling four-hour exam—she'd get a scholarship to the college of her choice.

Unfortunately, David was the only other Weymouth High student in the running. And he'd spent every spare second telling Aisha she shouldn't even bother studying. He claimed he could beat her with his calculator tied behind his back. In other words, Aisha hated his guts.

"Would you like some coffee?" Mrs. Gray chirped.

Aisha always thought of her mom as an African-American version of Martha Stewart. It was Mrs. Gray's passion for quaint inns and old-fashioned breakfasts that had led the family from Boston to this B&B in Maine in the first place.

Aisha stared at David. "I repeat, what is he doing here?"

Mrs. Gray calmly flipped a pancake. "I'm going to attribute this remarkable display of rudeness to sleep deprivation, Aisha," she said in her best we'll-talk-later-about-how-ashamed-you-should-be voice.

Aisha was now wide awake, but she moved toward the coffeepot anyway. "Excuse me," she muttered. "David, to what do we owe the pleasure of this unexpected visit?"

"David is Kalif's new math tutor," Mrs. Gray supplied.

Aisha almost dropped the World's Best Dad mug she was holding. "That's just . . . peachy."

"Isn't it?" David said, grinning.

Great. Wonderful. Super. Her archenemy was now infiltrating the home camp. The last thing she needed was to have the guy sucking up to her family with his fake charm. He'd sap out the support they were supposed to give her and use it to break down what little confidence she had left.

"How long have you known about this?" Aisha asked David, her voice dripping with sugary sweetness.

His grin widened to the point where Aisha began to hold out hope that his lip would split in two. "A few days."

"And it didn't occur to you to mention it to me?"

"Let's just say I didn't want to spoil the surprise," he said, leaning back and folding his arms across his chest.

Aisha turned back to her mother. "Kalif isn't getting tutored here in this house, is he?" she demanded.

Mrs. Gray nodded. "Yes, he is. David was nice enough to agree to take the ferry over a few times a week."

Aisha slammed her mug against the counter. "I think I'll go throw up now," she said.

As she padded toward the kitchen door, she heard David laughing softly behind her. "Happy studying," he called.

Aisha didn't answer. David Barnes was by far the most exasperating person she'd ever met. She couldn't remember being so irritated by someone since she'd first met Christopher Shupe.

As soon as she was in her room, Aisha dove under her covers. She was going to forget she'd gotten up that morning. She closed her eyes, trying to will herself back to sleep. But seeing David had set her nerves on edge, and her mind was jumping arbitrarily from one topic to another.

Aisha remembered when Saturdays had been fun. She'd wake up late, then go visit Christopher at Passmores', the restaurant Zoey's parents owned, in the afternoon. At night they'd hang out with the rest of the island kids, then make out in Christopher's small apartment. But her best moments with Christopher had been early in the morning, when he'd stop at her window at the end of his paper route.

Aisha laughed out loud as she remembered Christopher tapping on her window at five o'clock in the morning. Usually he'd been so cold that his teeth would natter during their first kiss of the day. But he'd never complained.

From the moment he'd set foot on the island the previous fall, Christopher had been determined to earn enough money to go to college. While she loved his drive and determination, ultimately those qualities had torn them apart.

When winter had set in, Christopher's cash flow had suffered. Out of frustration, he'd decided to join the army, where he could make money and get an education at the same time. And he'd wanted her to come with him.

Aisha cradled her pillow, remembering the devastated look on her boyfriend's face when she'd told him she couldn't accept his marriage proposal. For the millionth time Aisha wondered if she'd made the right decision.

True, she'd been madly in love with him. And she'd almost said yes. But after days of agonizing, she'd realized that she wasn't ready for a lifelong commitment. Especially one that would mean her leaving high school before graduation.

And now there was the Westinghouse competition. Since she'd gotten the news about being a finalist, she'd become a study machine. Her only form of entertainment was verbal sparring with David Barnes.

As much as she hated to admit it, the guy had a way of getting under her skin. Even worse, he knew it—and used the information to drive her stark raving insane.

Aisha groaned into her pillow. Men really, really sucked.

Four

Claire listened to the rhythmic groaning of the windshield wipers as she sped along the highway toward Weymouth. She usually got excited by rain or interesting weather of any sort, but that day she couldn't even summon the energy to scientifically identify the clouds overhead. Her mind was on Aaron. If the previous night had been different, she and Aaron would probably still have been lying together in bed. Maybe they'd even have been doing It.

"Jerk," Claire said through gritted teeth. "Idiot, moron, retard." And that was just her. The words she'd use to describe Aaron could lead to an arrest—or at least a restraining order.

"Be strong," Claire continued aloud. "Don't let anyone know he hurt you."

This was bad. She'd gone from practically pouring her heart out to a hotel employee to talking to herself. At this rate she'd be institutionalized by age nineteen.

Claire turned on the radio. Maybe some sound would drown out her own thoughts. The mellow voice of the DJ on WPOR immediately filled the car. "This tune's going out to Sweetie from Muffin," he crooned. "Sweetie says thanks for last night. It was one in a million."

Claire slammed her fist violently on the radio button. "Screw you, Sweetie," she yelled.

When she turned her eyes back to the road, Claire noticed a very wet-looking girl standing at the side of the highway with her thumb out. Without thinking, Claire put on the brakes.

As she got closer, she realized the girl looked to be about her age. She was wearing baggy jeans, a ski jacket, and a baseball cap, and she looked even more miserable than Claire felt.

Claire slowed the car even more. Her dad would have a fit if he knew she was contemplating picking up a hitchhiker. Not that she cared. He was off having a romantic getaway with the beast that had spawned her scum of a so-called boyfriend. It would serve Burke Geiger right to see on the five o'clock news that his elder daughter had been murdered by a psycho teenager from hell.

Claire pulled over to the shoulder, shaking her head. What kind of idiot chose to thumb a ride on a freezing cold morning in the middle of February, anyway?

Once the car was stopped, Claire rolled down the passenger-side window. "Where are you headed?" she shouted.

The girl leaned toward the car. "Weymouth."

"Are you armed?" Claire asked.

"Does this count?" The girl pulled a small can of Binaca breath spray out of her pocket.

Claire smiled. A hitchhiker with a sense of humor. Maybe this wasn't such a bad idea. "Hop in."

The girl smiled as she opened the door. "Thanks so much."

"No problem," Claire answered. She was glad the girl seemed as harmless close up as she had on the road. A carjacking would really have topped off her weekend.

"I'm Kate," the girl announced.

"Claire."

The girl shrugged off her jacket, which was soaking wet and already creating dark water stains on the soft tan leather seat.

"Thank God you picked me up," Kate said. She shoved her jacket on the floor and leaned back against the seat. "I got in with a trucker earlier. The entire inside of the guy's cab was covered with *Penthouse* centerfolds."

"You're kidding." Claire shuddered.

"I wish. I finally had him drop me off at a rest stop."

Claire laughed. "Sounds like an eventful morning."

"You're telling me."

Claire wasn't big on small talk, but Kate seemed cool. Maybe hearing about someone else's weekend would take her mind off her own. "So, what were you doing in Portland?"

"I went to a party. How about you?"

Claire felt a lump rise in her throat. "Same. Sort of."

Kate closed her eyes. "Man, I had a wild night."

"I hope it was better than mine," Claire said.

"It was amazing. I ran into an old friend. . . ." Her voice trailed off dreamily.

"Friend?"

Kate laughed. "Yeah, the kind of friend you wind up naked with."

Claire was surprised that hearing about her passenger's apparently steamy Valentine's Day wasn't sending her into a deeper depression. But Kate was so open and funny that Claire actually felt herself relaxing.

"So give me the details."

"Well, I hadn't seen him since last summer. Then bang, he was right in front of me. We started making out on sight."

Claire whistled. "Sounds explosive."

"It was. Until he remembered that his girlfriend was going to show up any second."

Claire's stomach suddenly sank to her toes. She was being paranoid. Irrational. Obviously this was a coincidence. "Really? His girlfriend?"

Kate sighed. "Yep."

"So, uh, what happened next?" Claire's heart was pounding painfully inside her chest, and she was gripping the steering wheel so tightly her knuckles were white.

"Well, to make a long story short, it turned out the girlfriend had already seen us. By the time we found out, she'd split. So we made the best of the situation and spent the night together."

Don't freak out, Claire. Stay calm. "Ah, do you mind taking off your cap?" Claire asked. Her voice was high and thin.

Kate gave her a strange look. "Why?"

"I'm just . . . curious about something."

Claire bit the inside of her cheek as she watched Kate's hand move in what seemed like slow motion toward the bill of her cap.

"Ta-da!" Kate cried. Her long red hair tumbled to her shoulders.

It was her. There was no doubt. Claire could never have mistaken that mane of curly red hair. Her life had suddenly gone from a mere nightmare to an episode of *The Twilight Zone*.

Without a word, Claire veered wildly toward the side of the highway. As she screeched the car to a halt, she tasted blood in her mouth. Until now, she hadn't noticed that she'd bitten through a couple of layers of cheek tissue.

"What's going on?" Kate asked.

"Get the hell out of my car." Claire reached past her and opened the passenger-side door.

Kate looked startled and slightly scared. "Jeez! What's your problem?"

"You know that friend you spent the night with?"

Kate still looked confused. "Yeah . . ."

"He's *my* boyfriend. Correction: *was* my boyfriend."

Kate grimaced. "Claire. Claire Geiger."

"Bingo." Claire turned her eyes away from Kate. The sight of her was making Claire sick.

"Oh, wow, I'm sorry."

"Get out." Claire gunned the engine to make sure Kate understood that she should get her butt out of the car. Immediately.

"You're going to leave me here? In the rain?"

"You got it."

Kate grabbed her jacket and got out of the car. Claire didn't wait for her to shut the door. She stomped on the gas pedal, letting the force of the car's momentum slam the door shut as she sped off.

In the rearview mirror, Claire saw Kate standing alone on the side of the highway. She looked cold. And wet. Watching the girl disappear into a small dark dot, Claire hoped the next person who picked her up would be a serial killer. Or worse.

It was almost noon by the time Benjamin made his way to the kitchen. His head was aching, and his mouth felt as though it were stuffed with a Brillo pad. Even the hair on his head hurt. Unfortunately, his condition wasn't anything simple, like a bad hangover. He was suffering the aftershocks of his rampage the night before.

When he got to the kitchen door, Benjamin heard the familiar sound of his sister making coffee. "The Terminator emerges," Zoey said from the counter.

Benjamin hung his head. "You heard about what happened last night, huh?"

"According to Nina, half the block probably heard," Zoey commented. "From her description, I gathered there was a lot of banging and crashing."

"Pour me some coffee, will you?" Benjamin mentally counted the three steps to the table, then found the back of a chair with his hand. Before his operation, he'd been so accustomed to navigating despite his blindness that walking through his house, the high school, and most of Chatham Island had been second nature. But since the bandages had come off and he'd discovered that he was still imprisoned in darkness, he'd lost the will to fight his disability. The day before, he'd even stubbed his toe on one of the legs of his own desk.

He heard Zoey set a mug down in front of him. "Sugar's at three o'clock," she said.

"Thanks." Benjamin was quiet as he carefully poured a couple of teaspoons of sugar into his coffee.

"Want to talk about it?" Zoey asked quietly.

Benjamin shook his head. He didn't know how to explain his actions of the past night. Furthermore, he didn't want to.

"Come on, Benjamin." Zoey sat down next to him, and he felt her hand on his arm. "Talk to me."

Benjamin put his coffee mug down with more force than was absolutely necessary. "I don't have anything to say."

"Do you, uh, want me to help you clean up?" Zoey asked.

"Someone's going to have to. I'm not exactly capable."

"Benjamin, you're not helping."

He shrugged. "Tell me something I don't know."

Zoey sighed loudly. "Do you want to hear what happened at the party last night?"

No, he didn't want to hear about the party. Did Zoey think he was a four-year-old who could be distracted by some inane anecdote about a large number of boring people? "No, thanks," he responded as politely as he could.

"Kate kissed Aaron," Zoey said anyway. "And Claire saw the whole thing."

Benjamin felt like screaming. "Do you think I give a damn, Zoey?" he shouted.

"You used to," Zoey said, sounding hurt.

Benjamin took a deep breath, then exhaled slowly. "I'm sorry, Zo. I didn't mean to snap at you."

"Don't worry about me. Worry about Nina."

Benjamin's stomach churned. Nina. He'd been trying to keep her out of his mind all morning. "You're right. Nina doesn't deserve the kind of treatment she's been getting from me lately."

"Finally, you're making sense," Zoey said. She sounded relieved.

"That's why I'm breaking up with her."

Zoey gasped. "You're what?"

Benjamin squeezed his eyes shut and forced out the words yet again. "Nina and I are through. As of now."

Lara

I'd start with a small nuclear bomb. That would probably take care of Kittery, my hometown. The only person I even remotely care about in that one-horse village is my mom. And she's done enough damage to my psyche that I wouldn't shed too many tears over her untimely demise.

After the bomb, I'd equip myself with one of those backpack-type things that exterminators wear when they're spraying your apartment for roaches. See, there's this long, thin hose that comes out of the side of the pack, and you hold it in your hand like it's a gun. Instead of common pesticide, I'd fill my device with some of those chemical sprays that Saddam Hussein kept threatening to use during Desert Storm.

Then I'd go find my old boyfriend, Keith. Not that finding him would be much of a task. He's serving one to three years in prison. That jerk stole most of my stuff, along with the couple hundred bucks I'd managed to save while I was living in Weymouth. While I was out shoulder-tapping—that's when you stop some hulking, smelly guy on his way into the liquor store and give him a few dollars to pick up something for you, too—Keith ransacked my apartment. He found the money under my mattress. Looking back, I realize that was probably a dumb place to keep it. I should have tried to find a loose floorboard or something.

Anyway, I'd point my little hose at Keith and spray him with my deadly chemicals. The loser would scream and whine and beg for mercy. I'd just laugh in his face and watch him die.

When I was done with him, I can think of a few other

people I'd like to give a good squirt, too, but they're hardly worth mentioning. I don't think I even have enough paper to list all their names.

I'm sure my lust for blood would shock my angel of a half sister. Zoey's idea of revenge is probably not smiling at someone on the ferry. Which brings me to another subject—my new family.

You might expect me to want some kind of revenge against Jeff Passmore. Let's face it—the guy shirked almost two decades' worth of fatherly duties.

But Jeff's actually a pretty good guy. And even though I know the rest of the family totally hates me, I kind of like them. Sometimes I even wish that Darla were my real mother. Not that I'd ever admit that to them. Ever.

Five

"What can I get you?" Lara McAvoy asked the gray-haired man who was sitting at table three in Passmores'. She was two hours into her shift, and things were not going well.

"I'd like a grilled cheese sandwich, an order of onion rings, and a bowl of clam chowder," he replied.

"Got it." Lara's stomach churned at the thought of the smell that would emanate from the kitchen when Jeff Passmore tossed onions into the deep fryer.

She went to the window that separated the main dining room from the kitchen and called in the order. "Thanks, Lara," Mr. Passmore said cheerfully. He tightened his short gray ponytail and gave her a thumbs-up sign.

Lara turned from his smiling face and sank into a chair. Sometimes it was still hard to believe that Jeff Passmore was her father. He was constantly smiling, and he seemed genuinely happy most of the time. Even when bad things happened, such as Benjamin's not getting his sight back, her dad maintained a positive outlook.

Lara rubbed her blue eyes, which felt as if they were ready to pop out of her head. For what seemed like the thousandth time since she'd pried her eyes open that

:ning, she regretted having drunk those last few shots
Jack Daniel's. At the time, the liquor had felt like
:edication. Now it felt like poison.

Her taste for alcohol was just one of many things that
made her stand out from her newly discovered family.
When Benjamin and his slightly crazy girlfriend had
tracked her down in Weymouth and told her that she
had a ready-made family waiting for her on Chatham
Island, she hadn't believed them. Then Jeff Passmore
had called and confirmed that he was in fact her long-
lost father and that he'd never even known of her ex-
istence.

In five minutes she'd gone from being the only child
of a single mother to being a part of the Cleaver family.
She still couldn't quite accept that Zoey and Benjamin
were her half siblings. They were so together. So perfect. The word *dysfunctional* probably wasn't even in
their vocabularies.

Of course, they'd hated Lara from the moment she'd
moved into the room over their garage. They couldn't
understand where she was coming from, and they didn't
want to. Zoey had practically jumped for joy when Mr.
Passmore had told Lara that she'd have to move to another place until she could learn to be a "responsible
member of the family."

Except for Jake, no one on the island had shown her
the least bit of kindness. And now that he'd become a
twelve-stepper, even he was trying to give her the
brush-off. Men sucked.

"Lara, order's up," Mr. Passmore called.

She dragged herself out of the chair and picked up
the tray of greasy food. Just as she'd feared, the smell
went straight from her nostrils to her unhappy stomach.

"Here you go," Lara said to the old man. She

put the food down as quickly as she could. *Ten, nine, eight* . . .

"Could you bring me some ketchup?" he asked.

Seven, six . . . "Sure. Just let me take care of something first."

She sprinted toward the bathroom. *Five, four* . . . She wrenched the door open. *Three, two* . . . She knelt in front of the toilet bowl.

One. Lara held her long, dirty-blond, somewhat tangled hair away from her face and puked expertly into the toilet.

One thing was definite: It was going to be a long day. By the time she got off work at five o'clock, she'd be ready for a drink.

Nina paced back and forth across her bedroom, moving her head in time with the Oasis song that was blaring from her stereo. A forgotten Lucky Strike dangled from her fingertips. In the last hour she'd developed a system. When she was pacing toward her door, she agonized over her failing relationship with Benjamin. When she paced toward her stereo, she tried to think of something useful to say to Claire.

Her sister had stormed into the house a little after noon. She'd headed straight for her room, and Nina hadn't seen her since.

It was now four o'clock, and Nina was halfway to the stereo. "Claire, I'm sorry that your boyfriend turned out to be as big a jerk as you are," she said aloud. No, that wasn't the approach she was going for.

"Claire, if there's anything I can do to help you in your time of need, just let me know," she tried, then shook her head. Claire would never buy a sappy line like that coming from her.

Nina reached the stereo and turned off the power. She

45

ouldn't stay in her room all night. Okay, she *could* stay in her room all night, but she'd feel like the worst sister in the world if she did.

As much as she ragged on Claire, the ice princess always came through for Nina when she really needed her. Like the time Nina had announced at a family barbecue that her uncle, who was visiting from Texas at the time, had molested her the summer after their mom had died. Or the time Claire had given Nina advice about dealing with Benjamin, even though he'd been Claire's own boyfriend for over a year.

Nina had to face facts. It was her turn to play the role of the loving, supportive sister. Yuck. Before she could reconsider her position, Nina strode out of her room and down the hall.

As she climbed the stairs that led to her older sister's third-floor bedroom, Nina whispered more opening lines to herself. "Claire, you want to talk? Claire, would it make you feel better to hit someone? Claire, do you want me to get you a fresh bag of human blood from your stash in the fridge?"

By the time she reached the top of the staircase, she'd settled on a simple hello. From there she'd have to wing it.

Nina knocked on the door. When she didn't hear Claire's distinctive growl, she went in anyway. She'd already figured that her sister had probably retreated to the widow's walk above her bedroom. Aside from her obsession with keeping an eye on developing weather patterns, Claire always claimed that the roof was the only place where she could really think. And Nina was positive that Claire was already up there, doing some heavy-duty ruminating.

Nina crossed the room and gripped the ladder that led to the widow's walk. "This too shall pass," she muttered as she heaved herself toward the small hatch that opened onto the widow's walk. Nah. Too biblical.

"Uh, hi," Nina grunted when she emerged into the freezing drizzle.

Claire was standing facing the ocean, her hands on the railing that went around the circumference of the roof, but she spun around when she heard Nina's voice.

"I guess you heard," she said flatly.

Nina took a couple of small steps toward her sister and tried to look ignorant. "Who, me? Heard what?"

Claire rolled her eyes, which were red and swollen. "Give me a break. You haven't been up here in months."

"Maybe I wanted a little fresh air." Nina inhaled deeply. "Ah, February. I love this month." She hugged herself, trying unsuccessfully to hide the fact that she was shivering uncontrollably.

"Or maybe you felt some perverse sense of sisterly duty and came up here to give me a lame bit of advice about how time heals all wounds," Claire responded.

Nina couldn't help but notice that Claire looked perfectly warm despite the fact that she was wearing only a yellow rain jacket over her jeans and sweater. "Zoey told me," she admitted.

"Good news spreads like the plague in this town," Claire said.

"Yeah, well, we both feel really sorry for you."

Claire smirked. "Gee, thanks, Nina. I'll savor that knowledge."

Wrong thing to say, number one. "I didn't mean it like that. . . ." She made an awkward attempt to pat Claire on the shoulder but jerked her hand away when she saw the look on her sister's face.

"In case you haven't realized it by now, let me be

47

the first to tell you that you're lousy at this," Claire said.

Nina felt real empathy sweep over her. She had first-hand experience with pain and rejection, and she knew how debilitating they were. And heartbreak was probably even worse for Claire than it was for Nina. Nina *expected* to be on the receiving end of hurt. Claire was accustomed to being the one holding the ax.

"Maybe there's an innocent explanation," Nina ventured.

"Yeah, and the earth is flat," Claire responded dryly.

"You never know—"

"I know," Claire interrupted. Her voice didn't leave room for any debate on the subject.

Nina tried again. "If it makes you feel any better, Zoey suspected from the beginning that Kate was bad news."

Claire narrowed her eyes. "What do you mean, from the beginning?"

Uh-oh. "You know, since she, ah, moved into the Cabrals' house."

"She lives with Lucas?" Claire shouted.

Nina gulped. "Claire, she's been there for, like, two weeks."

"She *has?*"

"Yeah. Her mom's an old family friend of Mrs. Cabral's. Kate just started at the art institute in Weymouth, and she's staying on the island until she can find a place on the mainland."

Claire slid to the surface of the roof and rested her back against the wrought-iron railing. "God, I've been in such a la-la land over Aaron that I missed a major piece of island news." She seemed to be talking to herself, so Nina didn't say anything. "I was just yapping away on the phone to him and writing ridiculous letters about how I couldn't wait to see him again."

"Well, Kate's kept a pretty low profile, anyway."

Claire glared at her.

Wrong thing to say, number two. "I mean, uh, she's been, uh . . ."

"Don't stand there stuttering on my account, Nina. No kind words from you are going to change what's happened." She paused. "Even if the words were halfway articulate."

Nina's energy was waning. Claire wasn't an easy person to talk to even under the best of circumstances. In this mood, she was about as touchy-feely as a death row inmate. Plus Nina was losing all feeling in her outer extremities. A good dose of frostbite was the last thing she needed.

"I guess I'll go in now," Nina said. "I think my lips are about to crack off my face."

"I'll see you later," Claire said. She'd already turned back toward the ocean.

Nina wondered briefly what her sister saw out there. Obviously it was a lot more than the cold, relentless gray waves that stared Nina in the face every time she gazed at the Atlantic. No matter how many years passed, Nina would never understand her sister.

Even though she was clearly desolate, Claire held her spine as straight as a broomstick. Nina observed Claire's still pride for a last second before she turned to leave. As infuriating as Claire could be, Nina admired her older sister. And yes, she loved her.

But Nina must have been insane to think she could offer any comfort. She and Claire had as much chance of becoming bosom buddies as Brad Pitt and Gwyneth Paltrow had of getting back together. Or Pamela Anderson and Tommy Lee had of having an amicable divorce. Nina thought for a moment. (She followed the rule of comic tautology, which called for funny things to come in threes.) Or Sonny and Cher having another top-ten hit on the pop charts.

All but Nina's head was down the ladder before Claire moved her head and looked directly at her. "Hey, Nina," she said softly.

"Yeah?"

"Thanks for trying."

Nina nodded. Maybe she was getting the hang of this sister stuff after all.

"And feel free to hit your head on the way down," Claire added.

Oh, well. Better luck next time.

The Top Ten Depressing Things that Happened in North Harbor on Saturday Night

10.

Lara ended her shift at the restaurant at 5:15 P.M. She then called Jake. Mr. McRoyan answered the phone and told her that Jake was at an AA meeting.

9.

At 6:00 P.M., Zoey made Kraft macaroni and cheese for dinner. Benjamin didn't want any, which turned out to be for the best, since Zoey realized after her first bite that the milk she'd used was *way* past its expiration date.

8.

Claire sat on her widow's walk until it got dark. Then she sat there some more. She finally went inside at 7:15 P.M., when she started to cry and her tears froze on her face.

7.

At 7:30 P.M., Aisha closed her advanced-placement biology book and tried to study chapter twenty of her two-inch-thick physics book, but in the middle of section two she became distracted by thoughts of how annoying David was. She slammed the book shut and went to the kitchen to make a batch of oatmeal cookies.

6.

At 8:00 P.M., Lucas arrived at the Passmores'. He told Zoey what had happened between Kate and Claire on the highway. Zoey said Kate deserved whatever she got. Lucas didn't agree. They argued. He left before they had a chance to make up—or make out.

5.

At 8:45 P.M., Aisha ate her sixth oatmeal cookie. She then called information for the phone number of Christopher's military base. When she finally got through, she was informed that Private Shupe wasn't allowed personal calls until after he'd completed boot camp.

4.

At 9:00 P.M., Nina arrived at the Passmores'. She found Benjamin in his room, which was still a disaster area. He reiterated the fact that their relationship was over.

3.

After Aaron's first call, Claire sat by the phone for two hours. She'd decided to at least hear him out when he called back again. But when the phone finally rang again, at 10:30 P.M., it was Mr. Geiger. He'd just called to tell the girls what a wonderful weekend he and Sarah were having.

2.

At 11:00 P.M., Jake took a cold shower. He thought about Louise's breasts the whole time he was under the spray, which rendered the effect of the ice water null and void.

1.

Lara polished off a half-empty fifth of Cuervo Gold tequila (which she'd snagged from Passmores' while Mr. and Mrs. Passmore had been discussing the possible purchase of new napkin dispensers) at a little after midnight. She then dialed the McRoyans' phone number but passed out before anyone answered.

LUCAS

When I first came to the island after getting out of Youth Authority (a euphemism for hell on earth), Jake McRoyan was out to get me. He basically ordered everybody not to talk to me.

I guess I had a few revenge fantasies back then. For instance, I wouldn't have minded breaking his nose and watching the blood spurt out. But I also felt sorry for the guy. First of all, his brother had died, which is worse than anything I can imagine. Then Zoey dumped him to go out with me, which was a form of revenge in and of itself.

After Jake found out that it was Claire, not me, who had been driving the car when Wade was killed, he dropped the silent treatment. Sort of. He still more or less hated me for going out with Zoey. But lately he's sort of mellowed out. WATER under the bridge, I guess.

Anyway, I'm glad I never broke Jake's nose. Partly because he probably would have done a lot worse to me in return, but mostly because it only would have made the situation worse.

That's why revenge fantasies are the kind of thing you should keep to yourself. I mean, look at Christopher. After some skinheads beat him up, he bought an illegal gun and went after them. If it hadn't been for Aisha, he would have killed one of those guys—and spent the rest of his life in real prison.

As of now, there's only one person who really makes me want to do something so crazy that I could wind up in jail. Aaron Mendel is the biggest weasel I've ever met. I wouldn't mind siccing a couple of the guys I met in the clink on him.

Zoey

There was a time when I was angry at my mom. I mean really angry. I'd taken the bus back a day early from a ski trip in Vermont after a huge blowup with Lucas over the fact that I didn't want to give up my virginity.

By the time I got home, I was exhausted, miserable, and generally disgusted with the human race. Little did I know that my mood was about to take a drastic turn for the worse.

I walked upstairs and heard noises coming from my parents' bedroom. When I say "noises," I'm referring to my mom's distinct giggle and a man's low, husky chuckle. Can you guess where I'm headed with this?

The low, husky laugh did not belong to my father. I peeked into the bedroom and saw none other than Fred McRoyan, Jake's dad.

At that moment, I think, I hated my mother. I can't remember ever having experienced such rage.

Later I found out that my mom's ridiculous fling with Mr. McRoyan followed her finding out that my dad had a love child with another woman he'd been involved with before my parents were married.

Anyway, as mad as I was at my mom, I can't say that I had an actual revenge fantasy about her. Basically I was just incredibly hurt, confused, and betrayed.

I guess my revenge consisted of giving her a huge guilt trip and freezing her out of my life for a while.

But in the end I realized my parents are human, just like everyone else. They do stupid things, which they later regret. Sort of like my period of temporary insanity when I fooled around with Aaron Mendel behind Lucas's back.

Lucas could have plotted revenge. Instead, he forgave me. Now, I try to view people's actions in the larger context of what's going on around them. True, I can still be overly judgmental and moralistic. But I'm working on it.

The next time I feel the need for revenge (and I'm sure that time will come), I'm going to try to take a good look at myself before I fantasize about wayward buses and "accidental" food poisoning at the restaurant.

What I'm trying to say is, "Let she among you who is without sin cast the first stone." Or whatever that line from the Bible is.

And if self-examination doesn't cure my need for revenge fantasies, then I'll write them down for use at a later date. Who knows? Maybe a good screenplay could come out of it....

Six

Zoey didn't want to wake up Sunday morning, but a persistent thumping on her bedroom door finally forced her to open her eyes.

"What?" she yelled crankily. The weekend had started off badly and proceeded to get worse. She had a feeling that the trend would continue.

"Room service," a deep, foreign-sounding voice answered.

Zoey smiled. The voice sounded a lot like Lucas's when he was making lame prank phone calls to her. "Come in, Lucas," she called.

"I can't," he said, shedding the accent. "My hands are full."

Zoey reached over the side of her bed and grabbed the thick red wool socks she'd kicked off during the night. "One sec," she called.

She pulled on the socks quickly, then braved the freezing cold of her hardwood floor. Who *was* it who had decided wood was charming while wall-to-wall shag was tacky?

When Zoey opened the door, her mouth dropped. Lucas was freshly showered and wearing khaki pants and a blue blazer. And he hadn't been joking when he'd said he was room service. He was holding a full tray of breakfast foods.

"What is all this?" she asked, stepping aside to let him in.

Lucas grinned. "You like?"

She waited for him to set the tray on her bed, then she slid into his arms. "I *love*," she whispered.

He gave her a long kiss.

"How do I taste?" she asked. Zoey hated morning breath, but Lucas never let it stop him from kissing her when he surprised her with a morning visit. Which was often.

"Like you could use some pancakes and maple syrup. And maybe a strip of bacon."

For the first time since she'd seen Lucas's beautiful face that morning, she remembered exactly what they'd been fighting about the night before. "Did Kate help you prepare this feast?" she asked.

Lucas didn't respond immediately. Instead, he went back out into the hallway. When he reappeared, he was waving a white napkin in front of his face.

"No, she did not help me," he said, still waving the napkin.

Zoey raised her eyebrows. "Lucas, may I ask what you're doing?"

"I'm waving a white flag. Calling for a truce. Holding out the proverbial olive branch."

She shook her head in exasperation, but she couldn't help laughing. Lucas looked incredibly sexy in his "waiter's uniform," his damp hair brushed back from his face. "Lay out the terms of the peace agreement, and I'll give it some consideration."

He set down the napkin beside the tray and slipped his arms around Zoey's waist. "I don't want us to argue about Kate anymore," he said simply.

"Well, I don't *want* to, either. It just happens."

Lucas sank onto the bed and pulled Zoey onto his lap. "Zo, there's nothing going on between Kate and me. There never has been and there never will be."

Zoey rested her head against Lucas's shoulder and thought about what he'd just said. There was a slight possibility that she'd overreacted in terms of Kate's desire to snare Lucas.

After all, Kate hadn't wasted any time dive-bombing Aaron the second she'd seen him. If she had really been interested in Lucas, she probably would have kept up the sweet big-sister act for another few weeks, then gone in for the kill once she'd gained his trust.

And it wasn't Lucas's fault that Kate Levin was a beautiful, incredibly talented girl. It wasn't as if he'd *asked* his mom to invite Kate to stay with them.

Most important, she hated fighting with her boyfriend. "Let's be friends," she declared.

He frowned. "Friends?"

Zoey brushed her lips against his. "Very, very good ones."

Lucas's arms tightened around her. "And you'll be nice to Kate?" he asked.

Zoey bit her lip. She still thought Kate was a jerk for spending the night with Aaron when she knew he had a girlfriend. Then again, it was just the kind of thing that Claire herself would do. And Claire didn't need Zoey to fight her battles. "Okay, I'll be nice."

Lucas shifted Zoey onto the bed and laid the tray on the floor. "I love you," he murmured against her neck.

Zoey's breath quickened as Lucas's lips moved gently across her neck. "I love you, too," she whispered. "But what about breakfast?"

He pulled his face away so that he could look into her eyes. "Experts say that exercise before breakfast is good for the metabolism." He kissed her again.

Zoey almost shouted with joy. Ever since Kate had come to Chatham Island, Lucas had stopped his campaign to get Zoey to relinquish her virginity. And as angry as she'd gotten at his out-of-control hormones in the past, his recent behavior had been making her insecure. Now it seemed that the old Lucas was back.

"Exactly how much exercise are we talking about?" she asked.

"Light to moderate."

"Nothing too strenuous?" she asked, running her fingers lightly through Lucas's hair.

"Promise," he said.

As Zoey kissed Lucas she forgot about breakfast, metabolism, and exercise. The only subjects on her mind were Lucas's warm lips and his (somewhat roving) hands.

By Sunday afternoon Nina had reached a new low in the realm of pathetic. But desperate times called for desperate measures. She finished dialing the 800 number bannered across the screen of the television set and waited for someone to pick up on the other end of the line.

"Healthy Living, Jenny speaking," a sickeningly perky voice said. "May I help you?"

"Uh, yeah. I want to order the Health Rider."

Nina's eyes moved back to the screen, on which a lissome young woman was achieving the "perfect workout" on an exercise contraption that looked like a cross between a mechanical bull and a stationary bicycle.

"Would you like to put that on your credit card, ma'am?" Jenny asked.

"Yes." Well, her dad's credit card. But what was a

little unauthorized use of an American Express Gold Card when buns of steel were hanging in the balance?

"One moment, please." Nina listened as Jenny punched something into what she assumed was a computer keypad. "May I have your credit card number and expiration date?" Jenny said a few seconds later.

Nina held up the card and squinted at the slightly raised gold-colored numbers. "Zero, one, four, four—"

Nina stopped reciting the digits when she saw Zoey suddenly appear at the doorway of the Geigers' den. "Hey, I came by to see how you're doing," Zoey said.

"Hold on, Jenny," Nina said into the phone. She covered the mouthpiece with her hand. "Great. I'm taking the first step toward improving my health and boosting my self-esteem," she said to Zoey, quoting the spokesperson from the Health Rider infomercial.

While Zoey stared at her, Nina gave Jenny the rest of her dad's American Express number, as well as her name and address. "Can I get that sent by express delivery?" Nina asked.

"Yes, ma'am, for an additional fee," Jenny responded.

"Nina, you're crazy," Zoey whispered loudly.

Nina ignored Zoey and finished her conversation. "I'm now the proud owner of a Health Rider," she said as she hung up the telephone.

Zoey rolled her eyes. "Nina, you've never exercised in your life."

"So what?" Nina said, shrugging. "There's a first time for everything."

Zoey switched off the television, where the toned young woman was still burning calories on the Health Rider, and sat down next to Nina on the couch.

"This sudden interest in gadgets that almost certainly

don't work has something to do with Benjamin, doesn't it?''

"Benjamin who?"

"Come on, Nina, out with it. Where does the Health Rider fit into whatever off-the-wall plan you've concocted to smooth things over with Benjamin?"

Nina thought for a moment. "Well, it's not the actual piece of equipment that fits into my plan. It's a state of mind."

Zoey raised an eyebrow. "A state of mind?"

"Yes. If I achieve firm thighs in thirty days, I'll feel better about myself. After all, self-improvement is the cornerstone of modern American philosophy." She paused. "Once I deal with the thigh issue, I'm considering a boob job."

Zoey laughed. "I think this is a little drastic."

"Hey, babe, whatever works." Nina turned the TV back on. She'd also been considering the purchase of a Wonder Mop.

"Personally, I think you'd be better off reading the latest issue of *Cosmopolitan*," Zoey said.

"Thanks, Zo. I'll take that bit of information under advisement. Now if you don't mind, I'm kind of busy."

As Zoey left the room Nina reached for the telephone. She'd decided that the Wonder Mop was a go. After all, it was really a mop *and* a sponge in one. And maybe she'd pick up Jaclyn Smith's line of cosmetics and facial cleansers as well. . . .

"Two points," George Wallace shouted. He threw a small Nerf basketball to Aaron. "Beat that shot."

Aaron glanced at his roommate. The guy had as much sensitivity as a vacuum cleaner. Aaron threw back the basketball. "I'm not in the mood, man."

Aaron gazed around the medium-sized room he and

George shared. George's sense of interior decorating was limited to posters of basketball stars and rock bands. He had three different pictures of Michael Jordan, as well as placards from the last two Lollapalooza tours. But the object George was most proud of was the bra he'd hung above his bed. Supposedly Cindy Crawford had worn it while shooting *Fair Game*, although Aaron had his doubts about its authenticity.

Aaron's side of the room was completely different. He had a seven-foot-tall bookshelf filled with classics, many of which were first editions. In the corner, his acoustic guitar had been carefully placed on a specially made stand. On the wall above his bed was a large map of the world as well as a map of the solar system like the one he'd given Claire for Christmas.

Aaron stared at the constellations outlined on the map. When he'd gotten Claire the present, he'd never even kissed her yet. He'd been too busy trying to conquer Zoey and sweet-talk her into giving him her precious virginity. Man, had he been stupid. Now that Claire was vowing never to speak to him again, he wished more than ever that he'd pursued Claire directly rather than wasting valuable time on her less interesting (though very cute) friend.

"Are you still mooning over that chick?" George asked.

"Claire's not a chick. She's a woman." Aaron slumped against the rickety wooden headboard of his boarding-school-issue single bed, feeling defeated.

"Whatever she is, she's not worth this much misery," George commented. He tossed the ball again, but it bounced off the rim of the miniature hoop they'd attached to their closet door.

Aaron rolled over so that his back was facing George. He didn't feel like engaging in a macho-fest. Sulking and self-recrimination seemed more appropriate. Aaron closed his eyes, picturing Claire. Man, was she good-looking. Any red-blooded American male would kill to go out with a girl like her.

"I want her back," Aaron said.

"Dude, there are, like, a hundred gorgeous girls on our very own campus. Why twist yourself into a knot over this chick—I mean woman—who lives, like, five hours away?"

"Have you ever *met* Claire?"

"You know I haven't."

"Well, then, you wouldn't understand." Aaron leaned over and picked up the Nerf ball, which had rolled under his bed. If he made this shot, he'd get Claire back. If not, he could look forward to a lifetime of lusting after his future stepsister.

Aaron threw the ball. It bounced off the rim and back into his lap. He took a deep breath. Maybe he'd go for two out of three.

Claire

I don't know if I'd call them fantasies, since I've carried out every plan of revenge I've ever had. They're closer to revenge realities in my case.

It's always been my policy to keep revenge on a practical level. A word here, a look there. Small gestures can work wonders when you're trying to ruin someone's life.

But I have to admit that lately my plans for revenge have taken a drastic turn. Ever since I saw Aaron kissing Kate, I've had dreams in which the most sensitive part of his body (I don't think I need to spell out exactly which portion of the anatomy I'm referring to) shrivels up and falls off.

Then there's the Lorena Bobbitt
scenario. A scalpel. A pair of sharp
scissors. Good lighting. I could make Aaron
into a permanent tenor in a matter of
seconds.

Seven

Claire was into her third hour of Sunday evening television. She'd taken over the den as soon as Nina had cleared out, muttering to herself about the wonders of interactive programming.

She was now watching *American Gladiators*, which as far as Claire could discern was a show in which people on steroids tried to climb walls, swing across rope ladders, and put little balls into strategically placed baskets while other people on steroids attempted to stop them. Claire was rooting for a gladiator named Diamond, who seemed to be the most ruthless of the whole bunch.

As Diamond clung to the foot of a woman who was dangling from something that looked like a bungee cord, the phone rang.

Claire's heart stopped. It was him. Every nerve in her body told her that Aaron had decided to make another attempt at explaining away his sleaze-filled night with Kate Levin. But this time Claire was ready for him.

She'd been hasty in her decision to hang up on him the night before. The silent treatment was too painless. She wanted to see, or at least hear, Aaron squirm. Maybe she could even have some fun. She muted the TV and picked up the phone on the second ring.

"Hello," she said coolly.

"Claire, please don't hang up," Aaron said. The words rushed out as if he'd been holding his breath.

"Hello, Aaron." She kept her voice neutral, as though there were a chance that she was ready to forgive and forget, or at least have a pleasant conversation.

"I'm sorry," he said.

The simple declaration caught Claire off guard. She'd expected him to immediately launch into some half-baked story in which he was the victim of a terrible misunderstanding. She took a deep breath.

"Oh? About what?"

"Claire, I know you saw me kissing that girl," he said, his voice shaky. "And I can explain. Really."

She should have known. Leave it to a guy to say one smart thing and then turn around and blow it. She'd overestimated Aaron's intelligence. "Can you?"

"Yeah. I was waiting for you at the party, totally excited. And then this girl came up to me . . . and just started kissing me. I tried to tell her I had a girlfriend, but she wouldn't listen."

"I assume you're referring to Kate Levin," Claire said icily.

"Uh, yeah," Aaron said. "Anyway, by the time I managed to break away, you were gone."

"How horrible it must have been for you," Claire said. Inside, she felt as though her stomach had turned to lead. But she knew she sounded as if she hadn't given the episode a second thought. Feigned indifference was a gift she'd always had.

"Yeah, it was. And now that you've had time to cool off and realize the whole thing was just a terrible misunderstanding, I hope we can make plans to pick up where we left off."

Claire almost laughed. Did Aaron really think she

wouldn't find out that Kate had ended up spending the night with him? He obviously didn't understand the nature of living on an island where people knew everything about one another—from who was getting a divorce to what time their neighbor peed in the morning.

Claire was about to lay into him for thinking he could get away with his one-night stand and live to date her again, but she suddenly changed her mind. As long as he didn't know for sure exactly what Claire did and didn't know, he'd be plagued with worry over whether or not she'd find out. If she was lucky, he'd even have nightmares about her running into Kate Levin on the ferry.

"Drop dead, Aaron," she said finally. Without waiting for a response, Claire hung up the phone.

Then she turned the volume of the TV set back up.

Diamond was in the lead.

Zoey Passmore was a genius. Nina slapped shut the issue of *Cosmopolitan* she'd snagged from Claire's bedroom, feeling better than she had since Benjamin had turned into the Incredible Hulk in his bedroom.

Nina couldn't believe she'd wasted the afternoon watching infomercials when she could have been gleaning pearls of wisdom from the pages of *Cosmo*. In the past, Nina had viewed women's magazines as messengers of the devil, but now she realized their importance.

She made a mental list of the articles she'd read in the last hour: "How to Keep Your Man Interested," "What to Do When the Magic is Gone," and "Winning *Him* Back."

After reading all three articles, she'd seen the answer to her problems with Benjamin as clearly as the ink on the page. She just had to do what any *Cosmo* girl worth her panty hose (or fatigues, in Nina's case) did when her man lost interest: make him jealous.

There was only one problem. Who was she going to make him jealous *with*? Nina went over possible candidates in her head.

There were lots of guys at school who lived in Weymouth who might work, but Benjamin wouldn't necessarily know that she was doing anything jealous-worthy with them. She needed someone who would definitely be around Benjamin and Nina together.

Which meant her decoy had to be an island guy. There was Lucas, but Zoey probably wouldn't appreciate Nina's cozying up to him, even in the name of love. Christopher was gone, so he was out. Kalif was cute and available, but several years too young.

Nina sighed heavily. Except for Jake, Benjamin was the only other decent guy on Chatham Island.

Nina's eyes popped open. Jake? No way. She shouldn't even think about it. She and Jake didn't even like each other. And he had the intelligence of a wombat.

Of course, Jake was the kind of guy who could make another guy jealous. Men were always envious of big, brawny jock types—even if they were recovering alcoholics who had somewhat unhappy home lives.

Nina glanced at the magazine again. She had to be bold. She had to be sexy and mysterious. She had to make herself seem attracted to a guy whose idea of a good time was running into other guys who were wearing tight pants and shoulder pads.

There was no question about it. *Joke* McRoyan was her man.

Jake didn't have to turn around to know who was knocking on the sliding glass door at the far end of his bedroom. For the past hour he'd been working on the list of goals for himself that Louise had suggested he make. But even as he'd stared at the computer monitor, he'd known in the back of his mind that Lara would show up eventually.

The week before, he'd told her that their relationship was over. He couldn't be involved with someone who had a drinking problem while he was trying to kick his own—he'd learned in the past that being around alcohol was too big a temptation. But Lara hadn't taken the news well. On Valentine's Day she'd left him a large box of smashed and half-eaten chocolates. He'd immediately stuffed the chocolates into his trash can, but he'd been haunted by the gift all weekend. Lara was totally unpredictable. For all he knew, her next so-called present could be an ice pick in his back.

Jake slid back his desk chair but left his computer on. He hoped to keep this confrontation as brief as possible.

As he walked to the door to let her in, Jake wished for the first time ever that his room didn't allow for such easy access from the outside. The McRoyans' house was built on a hill, and because Jake's room was in what would have been the basement, he had his own entry. When he'd been going out with Zoey (and Claire, for the five minutes they'd been involved), he loved being able to come and go without his parents' knowledge. But now he wished he could have his mom or dad run interference.

"Hey, Lara," Jake said as he unlocked the door and slid it open.

"Hi, Jake. Long time no see." As usual, she wasn't dressed warmly enough for the cold Maine winter. In a short denim skirt, knee-high leather boots, and a denim jacket, she looked like a Popsicle in the making.

"You really should borrow a down jacket from Zoey," Jake said.

"Are you kidding?" Lara said as she walked in and headed directly toward his bed. "Little Miss Muffet wouldn't let me near her stuff. She'd be too afraid of getting cooties."

Jake slid the door shut. When he turned around, he saw that the backpack Lara had dumped on the floor had a suspicious bulge. Despite himself, his mouth watered at the thought of the alcohol that was probably inside. He pushed the image out of his mind and pretended not to notice the telltale shape of a fifth of the hard stuff.

"Zoey's not like that," he said.

Lara unzipped her boots, then pulled Jake's comforter around her shoulders. "I'm not here to talk about Zoey," she said. Her voice held a warning tone that made Jake start to sweat.

He sat down in the large armchair beside his bed and tried to think of something to say. Nothing came to mind.

"Are you just going to sit there staring into space?" Lara asked.

Jake shrugged. "I guess I'm just not sure what to say," he responded.

"So don't say anything. Come over here and give me a kiss. For starters."

Jake bit his lip. There was no easy way to do this. He just had to come straight out and tell her that he didn't want to see her or hear from her unless she got her act together and came to an AA meeting. "I can't do that," he said quietly.

Lara stuck out her lower lip. "Didn't you like my Valentine, Jake?"

Jake shook his head. "Lara, I can't be around you anymore. At all."

She snorted. "Is this more of that AA crap you were spouting the other day?"

"It's not crap," he said hotly. "I don't want to drink or be around people who drink. It's not good for me." He paused. "And whether you can understand this right now or not, I'm not good for you, either."

Lara reached for her backpack. "I know what *would* be good for you."

Before he could stop himself, Jake yanked the backpack out of her hand, then strode back to the door. In a matter of seconds he'd slid the glass to the side and tossed the bag halfway across the back lawn. "I don't drink anymore. Period."

Lara flopped backward on the bed. When she spoke, Jake could hear real tears in her voice. "I don't want to lose you, Jake. You're the only person I have."

Jake felt his heart constrict. The aura of loneliness that surrounded Lara was what had drawn him to her in the first place. Well, that and her incredible legs. But he couldn't help her anymore. He needed to focus on his own well-being.

"Maybe you should reach out to your family," he suggested gently. "They're all great people."

Lara shook her head. "They don't want anything to do with me. Jeff's only keeping me on at the restaurant because he feels guilty for being a deadbeat dad all these years."

She sounded utterly defeated, and Jake had to force himself to stay planted in his chair. He knew that if he went to comfort her, a hug would lead to a kiss. And a kiss would lead to them spending the night together. He couldn't let that happen.

"Well, you've got to decide what's best for you," he said finally. "But all I can do for you is suggest you try an AA meeting."

Lara sat straight up on the bed and tossed the comforter aside. "You do whatever you want, Jake. But quit force-feeding me that twelve-step bull that's got you all hot and bothered. I don't need it."

Jake hung his head. "Maybe you'd better go, then."

Lara stood up. "Don't worry your wimpy little self, Jake. I'm leaving."

She stomped to the door and left without looking back. As Jake watched her ghostly figure move across the lawn toward her backpack, he felt a mixture of sadness and relief.

Sighing, he walked back to the project he'd abandoned when Lara showed up. Now more than ever, he needed to concentrate on the future. It was the only thing standing between him and that bottle in Lara's backpack.

<u>My Bottom Line:</u>
<u>Things that I, Jake McRoyan,</u>
<u>Will and Will Not Do</u>
<u>in the Near and Distant</u>
<u>Future</u>

1. I will not take a drink of anything containing alcohol.
2. I will go to an AA meeting every single day, even if I don't think I need to.
3. I will not blame other people for my problems.
4. I will make an effort to get to know myself better.
5. I will not blow off school, even if I feel like it.
6. I will go to college in the fall.
7. I will not drink when I go to college, even if it seems

like it's okay since everyone
else is.

8. I will try to have healthy
relationships (with both
friends and girlfriends) that
don't revolve around
drinking or codependent
behavior.

9. I will not get involved with
anyone who drinks to excess
(i.e., Lara McAvoy).

Note to myself: Add to this list
as I see fit. Maybe ask Louise for
more suggestions when I get a
chance to talk to her.

Nina

Do I have revenge fantasies? Ha! Does Dolly Parton have big boobs? Was Kurt Cobain depressed? Is Kermit the Frog green?

Sweet revenge. That's how it's always described in the grade-B TV movies they rerun on Lifetime every Sunday. (I'm having a vivid memory of Valerie Bertinelli-Van Halen, smoking gun in hand. "Ah, Sweet revenge," she says, laughing at the corpse of the pimp who kidnapped her and forced her into prostitution after she escaped an evil foster home.)

The hardest part about revenge is prioritizing. Who's more

deserving? The guy who wiped dog doo on your arm when you were six years old, or the girl in seventh-grade gym class who told you your breasts looked like mosquito bites?

Do I start with really big, like with my disgusting, pond-scum uncle who molested me? Or do I work my way up to the important stuff by starting with that driver who gave me the finger while I was at the wheel on our way to Vermont last winter?

So little time, so many people to torture.

If it came right down to it, I think I'd begin with whoever's responsible for planning the menu in the school cafeteria. It's probably some uptight, humorless middle-aged man on the school board. Let's call him Harry (it seems an appropriate name, since most of the food in the cafeteria is a little furry). I'd put Harry in a large, echoing room that smells of sweat, cheap perfume, and moldy turkey tetrazzini. Then I'd make him eat a whole week's worth of school lunches, from warm tuna surprise to cold Salisbury-steak special. After he puked (which he inevitably would), I'd make him eat that, too.

Eight

When Nina reached the *Island Breeze* (aka the *Minnow*) at 7:35 on Monday morning, she felt more alert than she considered healthy for an average junior in high school. But she had an important mission to accomplish. During the thirty-minute ferry ride to Weymouth, Nina intended to set Operation Make Benjamin Jealous into motion.

Nina felt her heart rate pick up as she entered the small interior of the ferry. Being manipulative was Claire's forte, not hers. She scanned the room quickly. Zoey and Lucas were huddled together in one corner, Aisha was studying in another. Benjamin was sitting in the middle on a long bench that was attached to the far wall of the cabin. Seeing him, she felt a fierce pang of acute discomfort. Nina stood still for a moment, trying to ascertain which seat would be most strategic.

"Hey, Nina," Zoey called. "Come sit with us."

Nina groaned inwardly. "Uh, no, thanks. I have some thinking to do."

"You can't think over here?" Lucas asked.

"Nope." Nina wasn't a good liar. The best way to avoid suspicion was clearly to say as little as possible.

"Where's Claire?" Zoey asked.

"Not coming," Nina answered. "Cramps."

"Is she okay?" Zoey asked. Her face had the concerned look that girls in secure relationships reserved for talking about other girls whose love lives had just gone down the toilet.

"Aside from being totally heartbroken and having a bad period, she's fine. Although I'm not entirely convinced that the cramps aren't just an excuse to sit in bed and ponder her hatred for Aaron Mendel. I didn't see any actual tampon wrappers in the bathroom trash can."

Lucas wrinkled his nose. "Why is it girls always offer more information than is strictly necessary?"

"Because unlike men, we view communication as a top priority," Zoey said.

"I'm not talking about *communication*, I'm talking about *information*. . . ."

Nina tuned them out. She knew from past experience that Lucas and Zoey would spend the next thirty minutes discussing the relative merits of telling or not telling the entire ferry that your sister has menstrual cramps. Which was exactly what she wanted. They'd be too engrossed in each other to pay attention to what Nina was doing.

More than anything, Nina wished she could forget her idiotic plan and go sit down next to Benjamin. Only a few weeks before, they'd used the morning ferry ride as an opportunity to make out. Now Benjamin was pretending that he didn't even know she was in the room.

Sighing, Nina draped herself across the bench that faced Benjamin's. She'd be the first person Jake would see when he showed up—*if* he showed up—which was exactly what she wanted.

Once she'd positioned herself on the bench, Nina looked down to check out her outfit. She usually picked out her outfits by sticking her hand in the closet and pulling out whatever her hand came into contact with. But that day she was wearing one of her few miniskirts, black tights, and a formfitting sweater that she'd inherited from Claire the previous winter when her sister's boobs had grown (despite what Nina thought was natural law) even bigger. She'd also put on about five coats of bright red lipstick, another first for a school day. Or any day.

As she tugged on her tights to smooth out her elephant ankles, Jake appeared in the doorway. She held her breath, waiting for him to notice her. He didn't.

Jake sat down on Nina's bench, but at the opposite end. She sat upright and slid toward him. She didn't have many opportunities to corner Jake, so she wanted to make use of every precious minute.

"Hi, Jake," she said, a little too brightly.

"Don't you mean *Joke*?" he asked.

Nina grimaced. It was no secret on the island that Nina didn't hold Jake's intelligence in the highest esteem—she'd called him Joke for years. But this was no time to dwell on the past.

She tried to laugh. "I've always loved your sense of humor."

Jake scratched his head, looking confused. "You have?"

She nodded, crossing her legs in what she hoped was a sexy manner. She'd seen Katharine Hepburn sit like this once, and the pose had seemed to drive Spencer Tracy into a lust-filled frenzy. "It's one of the things I've missed since you and Zoey broke up."

Jake slid a couple of inches away from her on the bench. "Whatever."

Okay. So her plan was off to a rocky beginning. She could handle it. She loved a challenge. Right. Well, actually she hated a challenge, but she didn't have much choice in the matter.

Nina moved over a little more to eliminate the space Jake had created. "You know, Jake, we've never really gotten to know each other."

He raised his eyebrows. "Nina, we've lived on the same island since we were born. How could we not know each other?"

Good point. "Well, yeah, sure, we know each other. But we haven't really *talked*."

Now he was looking at her as if she'd grown a second head. This was probably the longest conversation that Nina had engaged him in during the last three years. "What's there to talk about?"

"Oh, jeez, a million things . . . uh, the weather, school . . ." She should have thought about this problem in advance. For several seconds Nina racked her brain for a topic. "Basketball!" she finally shouted.

Out of the corner of her eye, she saw Benjamin tilt his head in her direction. Jake looked wary. "I mean, basketball," she said quietly. "How's the team doing this season?"

Jake lowered his head so he could look her directly in the eyes. "Are you feeling okay, Nina?"

"Who, me?" she asked, smiling so widely that she felt her upper lip curl under. "Why do you ask?"

"You don't seem like yourself."

Nina giggled. (At least she thought it was a giggle.) "How do I seem?" she whispered.

"Uh, sort of like you're coming down with a bad case of mad cow disease," Jake answered.

"Oh." Nina's heart sank. Her first attempt at meaningless seduction had been about as successful as *Waterworld*.

"And you might want to stop in the girls' room before homeroom," Jake continued. "You've got lipstick all over your teeth."

So much for sexy Nina. She stood up and laughed loudly for Benjamin's sake. At least *he* didn't know that she and Jake hadn't just had a scintillating conversation.

"Yeah, I'll see you later, Jake," she said loudly.

Jake gave her a hesitant smile. "Okay."

Nina sighed. No wonder Claire was in such a bad mood all the time. Trying to manipulate, use, and deceive people for one's own personal gain took a lot of energy.

Energy that Nina Geiger simply didn't have at eight o'clock on a Monday morning.

Benjamin sighed with relief when the bell rang. English was usually his favorite class, but that day it was just a reminder that Nina was out of his life. Since September, Nina had been his designated "reader." They'd fallen in love over boring chapters of American history and rambling Shelley poems.

But thanks to him, he and Nina were through. As a consequence, he hadn't done his English assignment. For the forty minutes that Mrs. Daily had been droning on about Franz Kafka, Benjamin had been thinking about Nina's soft, sometimes sultry voice. A voice that from now on he'd get to hear only in passing.

"Benjamin, may I speak to you?" Mrs. Daily called as he was making his way out of the classroom.

He grimaced. A well-meaning speech about how sorry she was that his surgery hadn't been successful was the last thing he felt like enduring. But teachers were teachers. When they talked, students had to listen. "Sure. What is it?"

He stood there, trying to look pleasant, while she cleared her throat. "First, let me say how sorry I am that your operation didn't turn out as you'd hoped—"

"Thanks for the concern, but I'm fine," Benjamin interrupted.

"Are you really?" she asked.

Everyone's a shrink these days. "Yes, I am."

He turned to go but stopped when he felt the teacher's hand on his shoulder. "Benjamin, we've got a problem."

We've got a problem? He was the one who was blind. What kind of problem did *she* have? "What?" he asked.

"Your grades," she said simply. "They've slipped quite a bit."

Benjamin gulped. He knew he'd missed a few assignments. And his final the previous semester hadn't gone well—he'd been too distracted by his upcoming surgery to give very articulate answers during his oral exam. But he hadn't given the matter much thought. He'd been too busy wallowing in self-pity.

"Well, uh, the junior who used to read to me has been pretty busy lately," he lied. "And I haven't found a replacement."

He could almost hear her nodding sympathetically. "That's too bad," she said.

He shrugged. "Yeah, well . . ."

"Benjamin, I've spoken to a few of your other teachers," Mrs. Daily said. Her voice sounded ominous. "And they've informed me that your grades are dropping in their classes as well."

Benjamin's heart sank. He'd worked his butt off for the past two years so that he could graduate with Zoey's class. He'd missed a whole year of school when he'd been sick, but he'd sworn to himself that he wouldn't let his little sister get a diploma before he did. "What are you saying?" he asked.

"If you don't get your act together, there's a possibility that you won't be able to graduate this spring,' she said.

He took a deep breath. ''I'll take care of it,'' he said. Before she could say another word, he spun around and found the door of the classroom with his hand.

His heart pounding, he walked down the hall to think. Almost immediately he came to a decision. He'd go to the principal and beg for mercy. Maybe he could get extra credit or retake a couple of exams or something. No matter what, he *had* to graduate.

Suddenly Benjamin stopped in midstride. ''Damn,'' he muttered under his breath. He'd been so focused on the demise of his academic career that he'd stopped doing a mental count of his steps.

Benjamin felt paralyzed. Surrounded by a sea of voices, he had no idea where he was. Well, he had some idea. He knew he was on the second floor of Weymouth High. He knew he was standing next to a row of lockers. But in his current situation, this information was essentially useless.

His heart raced as he stood perfectly still, trying to get his bearings. When no sound or smell distinguished itself, Benjamin had no choice but to accept that he was lost. He'd have to resign himself to asking some passerby for help.

''Excuse me,'' he said aloud. He waited for someone to stop beside him, but no one did.

Just as he was about to stick out his cane and catch the attention of the next unfortunate student to come along, he heard a familiar voice.

''Yo, Benjamin,'' Jake McRoyan said.

''Hey, Jake,'' he replied, trying to sound nonchalant. ''Uh, can you do me a favor?''

''Sure, man. What?'' Jake sounded so carefree that Benjamin felt like punching him in the face.

"Tell me where I am." Benjamin felt a blush rise to his cheeks as he waited for Jake to respond. He wasn't used to asking for help, and he hated it.

"You're across from Mr. Lancaster's room," Jake said.

Benjamin almost laughed. He had Mr. Lancaster the next period. "Point me toward the door, will you?"

"No prob." Jake put his hand on Benjamin's shoulder and turned him about seventy-five degrees. "Okay, you're good to go."

"Thanks, Jake."

Benjamin listened to Jake take off down the hall, then entered the classroom just as the bell was ringing. Before he had a chance to make his way to his desk, he felt a light tap on his shoulder.

"I'd like to talk to you after class," Mr. Lancaster said firmly.

Benjamin nodded, sighing. He wished that he'd never gotten out of bed that morning, because the day was obviously going to get worse before it got better.

Aisha

Revenge fantasies are about all I have going for me right now. The romantic fantasies sort of flew out the window when Christopher left.

Now as I'm lying awake at night, I think of ten different ways I'd like to make David Barnes wish he'd never been born.

There are the fantasies in which his fountain pen turns, James Bond style, into a bomb that explodes in his hand. His brain falls in pieces around the desk where I'm taking the Westinghouse scholarship exam.

My favorite form of revenge in that particular fantasy genre is the one in which he becomes suddenly allergic to math. Every time he looks at a logarithm, his face breaks out in this really disgusting rash. And when he uses a calculator, the tips of his fingers fall off. The best part is that when he tries to do long division in his head, his brain turns to mush. At the end of that fantasy, he's a pulpy mass of bone and flesh slumped over a desk.

But the revenge fantasy that I cling to is the one that might actually happen. It's boring compared to the others, but it's my favorite. The scenario is this:

David and I go in for the Westinghouse exam. We're both in top form as we sit down and start the exam. Four hours later, exhausted, we each hand in our copy of the test to the proctor.

Later David and I anxiously await the results in the principal's office. The grades come in. I've beaten David by a sizeable margin, fair and square. David's face is the picture of defeat, and I'm in the money.

Yeah, that one always makes me smile.

Nine

"A little late, aren't you?"

Aisha whipped her head around to face David Barnes. Behind his tortoiseshell glasses, she saw that his blue eyes were twinkling in the way she'd learned meant bad news. "Excuse me?"

She'd forced herself to go to the library right after school, but her nonstop studying was beginning to take its toll. After a fruitless forty-five minutes of staring at her biology textbook, she'd pulled out the still-blank Valentine's Day card she'd bought for Christopher.

"Your Valentine's Day card to Christopher," David said, as if he were explaining something to a four-year-old. "It's late."

Aisha frowned. "What do *you* know about Christopher?"

"Enough," David replied. He gave her a smug grin. "Your brother is full of interesting information."

Aisha made a mental note to kill Kalif before she went to bed that night. "FYI, my relationship with Christopher is none of your business," she said loudly.

"Don't you mean *ex*-relationship?" David asked. "And try to keep your voice down. This is a library."

The pencil in Aisha's hand snapped in two. "Being that you're a total nerd who's probably never even kissed a girl, you wouldn't understand the complexities of the thing we normal people call love," she whispered fiercely.

For a moment David looked hurt. Then the implacable mask came back, and he grinned. "Don't write anything too sappy. The guys at the base will probably pass your card around after lights out and read it under the covers with flashlights."

Aisha gave him her most superior glare. "If you ever got a card from a girl, I'd expect you to pass it around to brag," she said icily. "But as it is, I'm sure most of your illicit late-night activities are of the solo variety."

Aisha watched with satisfaction as a blush rose to David's cheeks. She now understood the expression "red as a beet."

"You're a vindictive girl, Aisha," he said.

She smiled. "I just call 'em like I see 'em."

David didn't have a response. He turned abruptly and walked toward his corner of the library. Score one for her.

She turned back to the card, feeling even more in the mood to send Christopher a belated Valentine after the unsettling encounter with David.

Dear Christopher,

Happy Valentine's Day. Sorry this is late, but I've been studying my brains out. I'm a finalist in a scholarship competition. The other finalist is a totally horrible guy who takes every possible opportunity to knock my self confidence into the academic gutter.

Anyway, I miss you more than you can imagine. If you were around, being your macho self, I'm sure David would be too intimidated by your presence to make half the cracks he dares to now. Still, I'm managing to hold my own, which I'm sure is no surprise to you.

Every day I question the decision I made not to get married to you (at least, not right now). But the possibility of this scholarship seems like a sign that I've done the right thing.

I still love you as much as I did the day you left. Please write and tell me how you're feeling. Your postcard was sort of a slap in the face, to be honest. I mean, couldn't you even have said "Dear Aisha"?

Anyway, I'm running out of room, so I'll sign off now.

Love, Aisha

PS Please don't show this to any of the guys there.

Aisha leaned back and read the card over. She'd had to write over the big heart that said *I miss you* inside it, but Christopher should get the point: She still loved him.

But when she read the card a second time, she noticed something different. She'd used more of her space to complain about David than she had to ask Christopher how he was doing. In fact, she hadn't asked Christopher anything at all.

Oh, well, she thought. That just proved to her what she already knew: that she detested David Barnes.

It was four-thirty in the afternoon, and Claire had just finished reading her third magazine, cover to cover. She'd started the morning with *Self* and *Vogue*. Then she'd watched several hours of daytime television, which had made her feel like a 1950s housewife from hell. At three o'clock she'd finally found her latest issue of *Cosmopolitan*, which had been lying on Nina's bed.

Claire tossed the magazine aside. As usual, the writing sucked and the articles were just a regurgitation of the previous month's issue. She lay back and closed her eyes. Maybe she really was about to get her period. PMS would explain why she still felt so totally miserable about the fact that a louse like Aaron Mendel had treated her like a common bimbo.

Claire groaned when there was a light tap on her bedroom door.

"Go away, Nina," Claire yelled. This concerned-sister act was getting a little old.

"It's not Nina," a voice answered.

Claire's jaw clenched. She recognized Kate Levin's voice instantly. Just like her flaming red hair, it was indelibly marked on Claire's brain.

"What the hell do you want?" Claire shouted.

"I'd really like to talk to you," Kate said.

Claire rolled out of bed. In a pair of faded blue sweatpants and an old Harvard sweatshirt, she knew she looked terrible. But she wasn't about to hastily run a comb through her hair to impress anyone, much less Kate Levin.

Claire opened the door just wide enough so that she could look Kate in the eyes. "I seriously doubt I'd find anything you had to say the least bit interesting."

"Claire, please." Kate was wringing her hands nervously. She looked as though she were waiting for a doctor to tell her whether or not the grapefruit-sized tumor in her brain was malignant.

Claire leaned against the doorjamb. "Fine. Talk."

"Can I at least come in?" Kate asked. She peered over Claire's shoulder into the room.

"I don't usually allow strange women into my bedroom, but I guess I can make an exception. We do, after all, have *friends* in common."

Claire opened the door wider, and Kate stepped tentatively into the bedroom. "This is a great room," she said.

Claire was gratified to hear a slight tremor in Kate's voice. Letting the girl say what she had to say on Claire's own turf seemed to have been a good call.

"Glad you approve," Claire said dryly. She sat down in her desk chair, leaving Kate to stand awkwardly in the center of the room.

Kate shifted from one foot to the other, then perched on the edge of Claire's queen-sized bed. "Thanks for not, like, punching me in the face or something just now."

"I'd have to give a damn about you to exert the energy to hit you," Claire responded coolly.

"Yeah, well . . ." Kate's voice trailed off, and she

averted her eyes from Claire's relentless stare.

"I'd appreciate it if you'd go ahead and make whatever little speech you prepared," Claire said after a moment of dead silence. "I've got things to do."

"I don't want you to hate me," Kate blurted out.

Claire laughed harshly. "Kissing my boyfriend wasn't the best way to get on my good side."

"I didn't even *know* Aaron had a girlfriend when I saw him at the party—"

"Until he told you," Claire pointed out. She hadn't forgotten that Kate had spent a sex-filled night with Aaron even after she knew that he belonged to someone else.

"I know I said it before, but I really am sorry," Kate said. "If I'd met you before the whole thing ever happened, I never would have fooled around with him."

"Is that so?" Claire asked. She didn't know what Kate expected her to do. She wasn't about to shake hands and chalk the whole thing up as a mistake. Claire fully intended to hold a grudge—forever.

"Yes," Kate insisted. "It's just that I was so in love with Aaron last summer. . . ."

"How touching." Claire picked up *Self*, which was lying on her desk, and began flipping idly through the pages.

Kate shrugged. "I guess I still am."

"Still are what?" Claire asked. She looked up quickly from a Gap ad featuring a tattooed woman in khakis.

"In love with Aaron."

Talk about pathetic. Claire shut the magazine. "You can have him," she said. "Unlike girls with less self-esteem, I don't like used goods."

Kate grimaced. "I guess I deserved that."

"I'd say so," Claire responded. "Now if you've had

your say, I'd like to get back to what I was doing." *Which was absolutely nothing*, she added silently.

Kate nodded and took a step toward the door. Then she hesitated. "I hope we'll be able to put all this behind us," she said, giving Claire a small smile. "I think you and I have a lot in common. I mean, we already know we have the same taste in guys." She tried to laugh, but the sound that came out of her mouth sounded closer to a sob.

Claire arched one perfectly plucked eyebrow. "I hope you're not suggesting that you and I could actually become friends."

Kate smiled again. "Stranger things have happened."

"Yeah. To Dorothy and Totó in *The Wizard of Oz*," Claire replied.

Kate looked at Claire for a moment longer, then let herself out of the bedroom. As Claire listened to her footsteps fade down the stairway, she felt surprised.

Because despite herself, she didn't hate Kate. She even admired the nerve Kate had demonstrated by facing Claire one on one. For a brief moment Claire wondered if maybe there was a chance that the two girls could become friends.

Then she shook her head. Nope. That would interfere with her plan to hold a grudge—forever.

JAKE

I used to be pretty big on revenge. Like with Lucas Cabral. For over two years I thought he'd been driving drunk the night my brother, Wade, died in the car accident. While Lucas was away at Youth Authority, I'd lie in bed and think of how much I wanted to strangle the guy.

When he came back to Chatham Island, I insisted that no one speak to him. I wanted him to be a total pariah—sort of like Cain, I guess. But all of my anger got me exactly zip.

Zoey felt sorry for the guy (girls are like that), which eventually led to her falling head over heels for him. She dumped me without a second thought. Talk about revenge fantasies! Man, I really wanted to get Lucas then. I think revenge would have included some gasoline and a blowtorch.

Then it turned out that Lucas hadn't been driving after all. It was Claire who had been behind the wheel. Lucas had covered for her because he was in love with her, if that makes any sense. Unfortunately (or fortunately, depending how you look at it), I was in love with Claire when I found out this piece of information.

I was pretty broken up for a while, but I never wanted to

strangle Claire or hang her up by her toenails. I just felt like crying.

Since I've been in AA, I've realized that most of my anger was really directed toward Wade. How could he have gotten stinking drunk with Claire and Lucas, then climbed into a car? I mean, he wasn't even wearing a seat belt.

I don't know if I'll ever be able to totally forgive Wade for dying, but I'm getting there. And I've given up most of my revenge fantasies.

In the long run, they don't do any good. When it comes right down to it, wasting your energy hating other people kinda makes you hate yourself.

BENJAMIN

Revenge? Sure, I have a few thoughts on the subject. But my revenge fantasies don't involve a person. They center around a disease.

Thanks to some mutating virus, I lost my sight. But fighting against something in your own body is basically impossible. I mean, I'm not going to tear my own eyes out.

And even if I'd been blinded by a person—say, if Mike Tyson had given me a left and then a right to the eyeballs, or I'd been shot by an armed robber—I'd still be powerless.

A blind guy walking around with a thin white cane and a pair of black Ray-Ban sunglasses isn't the most threatening presence.

So I have to stick more to the fantasy part of it than to the revenge part. For the last few years, my fantasy was that I'd wake up one morning and be able to see.

When I had my laser surgery a couple of months ago, I actually brushed up against my dream, the way other people have brushes with death. Being that

close to my fantasy, and having it not
come true, made cold, hard reality that
much crueler.

Now I have nothing. Not even a wish.

Ten

Zoey banged her tray down on the cafeteria table, where Claire and Aisha seemed to be studying their food as if it were a lab experiment rather than a meal.

"I've got to do something," Zoey declared.

Aisha looked up from her turkey burger. "About what?"

"Benjamin."

"I don't think there's much you can do, Zoey," Aisha said. She moved her tray to the side and picked up her carton of skim milk.

Claire nodded, then followed Aisha's lead by pushing her own tray to the far end of the table. "Aisha's right. Benjamin's going to have to work through this on his own."

Zoey wasn't surprised that Claire was acting as calm and collected as she always did. Spending lunch crying over a boyfriend's infidelity wasn't her style. As always, Zoey was impressed by Claire's ability to behave as if she didn't have a care in the world. She even looked genuinely concerned about Benjamin's well-being.

"He's my brother," Zoey said, taking the bun off her burger and smothering the thin patty with ketchup. "I can't just sit back and let him throw his life away."

Since he'd informed her that he'd called it quits with

Nina, Benjamin had barely said two words to her. Zoey wanted to talk to her parents about his obvious depression, but they'd both been putting in even more hours than usual at the restaurant since Christopher had left. Every time she saw them, they were either headed to or from bed.

"He'll snap out of it eventually," Claire said. "Benjamin's too smart to let himself stay depressed forever."

"The guy's almost twenty years old," Aisha pointed out. "He's old enough to let himself wallow in self-pity if he wants to."

Zoey snapped her fingers. "That's it!"

"What's it?" Aisha asked.

"Benjamin's birthday is February twenty-eighth." Zoey took an ambitious bite of her turkey burger, then promptly spit it out into her napkin. She picked up the tray and placed it next to Claire's.

"So?" Claire asked.

Zoey cleansed her mouth with a large gulp of lemonade, then beamed at her friends. "So we'll have a surprise party for him."

"Oh, no," Aisha said quickly. "Surprise parties are not good."

"Aisha's right," Claire said. "The person who's getting surprised either finds out about the party in advance or ends up resenting the party-giver for making him face a bunch of people without proper mental preparation."

"Benjamin will hate you," Aisha agreed.

"You guys have no sense of adventure," Zoey said. Now that she'd come up with the idea, nothing was going to stop her. "Nina will think it's a great idea."

"Nina lost *her* mind years ago," Claire said.

"Hey, where is she, anyway?" Zoey asked. She'd been so focused on Benjamin that she hadn't even noticed Nina's conspicuous absence from the table.

"Don't look now, but she's sitting with Jake," Aisha answered.

Zoey immediately turned her head. Nina sitting with Jake was like Newt Gingrich playing golf with Bill Clinton. It just didn't happen. "Where?" she hissed.

Claire pointed toward the far corner of the room. "Right there."

Zoey couldn't believe it. This was the second time that day she'd seen Nina engaged in conversation with Jake. "There must be something even stranger than usual in the food," she said.

"I think our little Nina has been reading *Cosmopolitan*," Claire said.

Aisha glanced toward Nina and Jake, then back at Claire. "What does that mean?"

Claire smiled enigmatically. "I think it means that very soon we're going to see Nina make a top-notch, grade-A ass out of herself."

Zoey plucked a chocolate chip cookie from her tray and took a bite. She didn't have time to worry about why Nina suddenly found Jake a stimulating conversationalist.

She had a surprise party to plan.

"What're you doing here?" Lara McAvoy demanded.

"Last time I read the Constitution, blind people had just as much right to a cup of coffee as anyone else."

"Touchy, touchy," Lara said. Benjamin resisted the urge to accidentally hit her in the head with his cane.

After school Benjamin had gone straight to Passmores'. The prospect of going home and listening to what was left of his CD collection for the next six hours had been too depressing even to contemplate.

He also felt incredibly guilty. He'd fully intended to

go to the principal's office that afternoon and state his case, but he'd never gotten around to it. After years of being Benjamin the blind wonder boy, it was going to be harder than he'd imagined to admit defeat.

"Just get me the coffee," Benjamin snapped.

Lara had a knack for irritating the hell out of him. When he'd first met his half sister, he'd hoped that they would become friends. That hope had diminished quickly when she'd moved into the room above the Passmores' garage. Her almost daily comments about his blindness had made him feel like a circus freak. Since she'd moved out of the house and into Christopher's old room in the boarding house, he'd run into her only a few times.

He heard Lara return a minute later. "Here you go," she said. "It's right in front of you."

"Thanks." Benjamin found the handle of the coffee cup and took a sip. He assumed that Lara would retreat to the other side of the restaurant, but he didn't hear her walking away.

"Do you want something?" he asked.

"A little conversation would be nice."

"I'm not going to be very good company," Benjamin said. "You'd be better off filling the sugar bowls or rolling napkins or something."

Go away, he said silently. He took another sip of coffee and shifted his blank gaze in the opposite direction from where he knew she was standing. Eventually she'd get the point.

"What's wrong?" she asked, sitting down in the chair next to his.

Leave it to a girl to ask exactly the wrong question. "I'm blind. I broke up with my girlfriend. And I'm flunking out of school. How's that for starters?"

"Jeez, your life sounds even worse than mine," Lara said. As usual, her tact was priceless.

"Believe me, it is." Benjamin took a gulp of the quickly cooling coffee. The idea that he was even worse off than his half sister was truly frightening.

"So how come you're flunking out of school?" she asked.

"Because I haven't done any of my assignments in weeks. Nina used to read to me, but now that I've dumped her, I can't exactly ask her to come over and help me with my homework."

Benjamin was appalled that he was spilling his guts to Lara. She was, however, the one person who could probably relate to being in a seriously cruddy situation. Her whole life was one cruddy situation after another.

"I'll do it," Lara said when he didn't continue.

"Do what?"

"Read your assignments."

"You?" The thought of Lara as his personal study guide was beyond absurd.

"Yeah, me. I *can* read, you know." She sounded hurt.

"Sorry. I'm just surprised you'd want to do something like that."

He heard Lara stand up and move away from the table. "Listen, do you want me to do it or not?"

Benjamin adjusted his blind gaze in the general direction of where he thought she was standing. "Uh, yeah, sure."

Why not? It was either that or burden Zoey. And Zoey had to pick up enough of his slack as it was.

"Fine," Lara said. "Come over tomorrow night at seven."

Benjamin felt like banging his head against the table as he listened to her walk away. His life had come down to a study date with his crazed, alcoholic half sister.

This was definitely a manifestation of Murphy's Law: If anything can go wrong, it will.

Jake was still damp from his post-basketball-practice shower when he slid into a chair at the back of room 401 in Weymouth High. He'd never had an actual class in this room, but since he'd started going to AA meetings, the place felt like home away from home. A dysfunctional home, but a home.

As soon as he'd taken off his jacket, he scanned the room for Louise. They usually sat next to each other during meetings, but he hadn't seen her when he'd first walked in.

"Hi, Jake," she suddenly called.

She was sitting at the front of the room, in the chair that was designated for whichever person was leading the meeting. Every day someone different spoke about their experience with alcoholism. Jake always felt shaken after the person spoke—or told about their experience, strength, and hope, as it was called in AA. But he could almost always relate to at least part of what the person had to say. And the act of listening, really listening, to another person's story had taught him more about himself than he'd ever thought possible. Once or twice he'd even had to fight back tears—especially when the person speaking happened to mention the death of a family member.

Ron Stade, who often chaired the meeting by saying a few words and then introducing the speaker, stood up. "Okay, everyone, settle down," he called.

Instantly the room became quiet. As Ron rattled off the rules and philosophy behind Alcoholics Anonymous, Jake stared at Louise. He'd known she was approaching ninety days of sobriety, when a recovering alcoholic became eligible to speak. But he'd never considered the possibility of her actually leading the meeting.

As Ron turned to Louise, Jake felt nervous. He knew that he was about to hear a side of Louise Kronenberger that had remained shielded from him despite their newfound friendship. And he wasn't sure he was ready for it.

Jake took a deep, steadying breath, then leaned back to listen to what the girl with whom he'd lost his virginity had to say.

"Hi, my name is Louise, and I'm an alcoholic," she said.

"Hi, Louise," everyone in the room, including Jake, chorused.

And then she proceeded to tell her story. . . .

Louise's Experience, Strength, and Hope

I had my first drink at a cousin's wedding. It wasn't whiskey or anything. I just snagged a glass of champagne from one of the adult tables. Anyway, I was thirteen at the time, and I didn't even like the taste. I didn't get drunk that night, although I remember giggling a lot.

And the whole wedding reception seemed like magic. Everyone was laughing, and by the end of the night my parents were dancing real close. Most of the time they were at each other's throats, which is why the dancing made such an impression on me.

The summer before ninth grade, my parents split up. Even though they'd hated each other most of the time for as long as I could remember, I was still totally devastated when they separated. And back then I was this shy little kid who wore glasses and read books all the time. I was the tallest girl in the class, but my chest was flat as a pancake.

Then ninth grade hit. I was still shy and a geek, but my breasts shot out like torpedoes. I mean, overnight I went from a 32A to a 36C. At least it seemed like it was overnight.

One night in October, my mom dropped me off at a Weymouth High football game. She was going to this singles group, and she didn't want me to sit around the house sulking, the way I usually did on Friday nights.

Anyway, I was sitting alone in the bleachers. I had no friends, and I felt totally uncomfortable. But then these four senior guys sat down right in front of me. They were passing around a brown paper bag of something—vodka, I found out later. Then one of them—his name was Trent—started talking to me.

I was so freaked out that this cute senior was even giving me the time of day that I just sat there stuttering. Until he passed the brown bag in my direction. I took a huge gulp of the stuff, just to look cool, and I came damn close to throwing it right back up. Instead, I just breathed deeply until the nausea went away.

Pretty soon the bag came my way again. I took another gulp, and this time it wasn't so hard to swallow. And I was starting to feel good. I mean, really good. I moved down a row and sat sandwiched among those four guys, feeling like the belle of a southern ball.

After my third or fourth swig, my tongue loosened up. I was cracking jokes, flirting, and generally feeling like a million bucks. I mean, these guys were, like, hanging on my every word. At least that's how it seemed at the time.

When the game ended, we all got in Trent's car. By that time, I was so smashed that they practically had to carry me to the parking lot. But no one seemed to mind. They were laughing and calling me Fun Louise.

Trent dropped the rest of the guys off, then parked the car at the end of a dead-end street. My head was spinning, and I was worried what my mom would think when I didn't come home right after the game, but I still felt like a princess. I didn't want the night to end.

I just sat there while Trent smoked a cigarette. My heart was beating a mile a minute, and I was taking in every little detail of the situation so I could replay it later in my mind. I still remember the way the smoke from the Marlboro curled around his head after he exhaled. . . .

Finally he kissed me. I figured that after a few minutes he would stop. I was only fourteen, and the sum total of my experience with sex had been a peck on the lips during a game of spin the bottle in seventh grade. But he didn't stop, and I just sat there, kissing him back.

To make a long story short, I lost my virginity that night. When I got home at three A.M., my mom was watching TV in her bathrobe. At first she was furious. She said she'd been ready to call the police. But I'd sobered up a little by then, and I gave her a heavily edited version of what had gone on. I made sure I stayed far enough away from her so that she couldn't smell the alcohol on my breath. She never suspected a thing.

When I finished the story, she was actually proud of me. Her daughter the bookworm had met a cute older boy. It was like a fairy tale. She just said I should call if I was going to be late from now on.

Trent wouldn't talk to me on Monday, and I was crushed. But news about a girl who puts out spreads fast. By Friday, I had two dates lined up for the weekend. I didn't care who I went out with as long as I could be Fun Louise again. And I was. Again. And again. And again.

You can probably guess the rest. I went out every weekend with virtual strangers. I'd drink until I could turn into Fun Louise, then I'd have sex. Pretty soon I got smart enough to bring my own condoms along, but that's about the only even semi-intelligent thing I did for three and a half years.

I became the class slut. Nice girls wouldn't talk to

me, and nice guys would be friendly only if we were in the backseat of their car or holed up in some empty room at a party. It was always wham, bam, thank you ma'am.

But I didn't care. Whenever I felt bad about my life, I'd just shoplift a bottle of something and drink myself into oblivion.

But three months ago my mom found me passed out on the floor of my bedroom. When she couldn't wake me up, she took me to the emergency room. They pumped my stomach and told her I could have died from alcohol poisoning.

For some reason, I told my mom about what had been going on in my life—well, most of it. She was in shock. That night she just cried. But the next morning she took me to an AA meeting that the doctor had told her about. I haven't had a drink since.

I've been sober for ninety days now. Every day is a challenge, but every day I feel a little more like the Louise who's been waiting to come out for the past seventeen years.

Someday I may even be able to look in the mirror and see more than Fun Louise. More than the class slut. More than a pair of boobs and a mouth built for guzzling alcohol. Every time I want to take a drink, I think of that naive little girl at the football game. And every time it's she who prevails. . . .

Jake was dimly aware that Louise had stopped talking. His left leg had fallen asleep, and his eyes were burning because he hadn't blinked for at least fifteen minutes.

As soon as Louise had opened her mouth to begin telling her story, Jake had been mesmerized. Louise Kronenberger had always seemed made of steel. She'd laughed off the most brutal insults with a pint of beer and a one-night stand. Even since he'd gotten to know her through AA, Jake hadn't really bothered to peel back the layers and find what lay beneath the reputation.

Now he felt engulfed with shame. He'd been one of those nameless, faceless guys who'd thought of Louise as nothing more than an easy lay.

But what was even weirder than his latent guilt about how he'd viewed Louise all these years was a sense of wonder. As he'd listened to Louise's raw, uncensored story, he'd realized she was one of the bravest women he'd ever met.

Scratch that. She was one of the bravest *people* he'd ever met.

Eleven

Claire had thought that over the last few days she'd been as miserable as a person could be. But her isolated state of humiliation and despair had been nothing compared to this dinner.

Mr. Geiger and Sarah Mendel had specifically requested a so-called family dinner so that they could share their wedding plans with Nina and Claire. Only five minutes into it, Claire felt like a reject from the Brady Bunch.

She speared a piece of asparagus with her fork and forced herself to put it into her mouth.

"So, how was the party last weekend?" Mr. Geiger asked.

Claire swallowed the asparagus without chewing. "Oh, fine. Terrific."

"My weekend blew," Nina commented to no one in particular.

Mrs. Mendel gave Nina a look that said *I can't believe this freak is going to be my stepchild*, then rested her hand on top of Mr. Geiger's. "Well, your father and I had an absolutely fabulous weekend."

Claire wondered if her throwing up on the dinner table would be a sufficient deterrent to Sarah Mendel's deciding to become the second Mrs. Burke Geiger.

"How neat," she said, pasting a Colgate smile on her face.

"Late breakfasts, long walks in the afternoons, roaring fires at night . . ." Mrs. Mendel sighed happily.

"I hope you two kids were careful," Nina said.

"Careful?" Mrs. Mendel asked.

"Nina's trying to make a very tacky joke about safe sex," Claire interjected.

"Oh! Well, my," Mrs. Mendel said, a blush rising to her cheeks.

Mr. Geiger cleared his throat. "That aspect of our lives is less than none of your business," he said sternly.

Claire sensed hysterical laughter bubbling up within her. She felt as if she'd entered the theater of the absurd. While her boyfriend had been boinking Kate Levin, his mom had been boinking Claire's dad. And now they were talking about it over roast beef and mashed potatoes. It was all *so* nineties.

"Anyway, we made some wonderful wedding plans," Mrs. Mendel continued, as if the incredibly awkward moment had never happened.

"We're going to have the ceremony right here on the island," Mr. Geiger said.

"And I'd be honored if you two girls would be my bridesmaids," Mrs. Mendel said. She beamed at Claire and Nina as though she'd just offered them the crown jewels.

"I plan to ask Aaron to be my best man," Mr. Geiger added.

Claire stared at her dad and his future bride with her mouth agape. This was too much. Really, just too much.

"Wow, a real family hoedown," Nina said.

"Claire, don't you have anything to say?" her dad inquired.

Claire swallowed hard, trying to regain her composure. She opened her mouth to say something, anything, but no words came out.

In the kitchen, the telephone rang. *Saved by the bell*, she thought.

A moment later Janelle, the Geigers' housekeeper, poked her head into the dining room. "Sarah, telephone for you," she said in her thick Maine accent.

Mrs. Mendel disappeared into the kitchen. In her absence, Claire, Nina, and Mr. Geiger stared at each other in silence. Claire was sure that the caller was Aaron. Who else would know to get in touch with his mother at their house?

Her stomach, which was already in knots, churned. She couldn't believe that louse was going to be her father's best man. Not to mention her own stepbrother.

Claire shook her head. She had to stop this madness. Some way, somehow, she was going to derail this marriage. Even if she had to resort to lies, cheating, and trickery to do it.

In less than a minute Mrs. Mendel was back. "Aaron's on the phone," she chirped in her most saccharine, singsong voice. "And he wants to speak to Claire."

Claire smiled for the first time all night. Of course. Aaron Mendel, master of deceit, was her ticket. Maybe he was good for something after all.

"Oh, good," Claire said pleasantly. "I have a few things I'd like to say to him as well."

Claire walked into the kitchen, eagerly anticipating her date with the devil.

Aaron was surprised that Claire had agreed to come to the phone. Maybe this was a sign that she was caving. After all, she couldn't resist his charms forever.

"Perfect timing, Mendel," Claire greeted him.

"Hello to you too, beautiful."

"Don't even think about using this phone call as a pathetic attempt to worm your way back into my life," she said bitterly. "We have important business to discuss."

Okay. So she wasn't quite ready to kiss and make up. Even getting her to talk to him was a big step forward. He'd just have to make the best of it. He lay back against the pillows on his bed, cradling the receiver as if it were Claire herself.

"I'm all ears," he said.

"At this moment our parents are planning their wedding," Claire said darkly.

Aaron laughed. "I don't know about you, but I can't wait for the blessed event."

He heard a gagging sound at the other end of the line. "You can't be serious."

"I'm totally serious," he responded.

He'd already had about a hundred fantasies about the wedding night. While Mr. Geiger and his mom were jetting off to some tropical island, he'd be cozying up to Claire in her very own bed. What could be more ideal?

"Listen, Aaron, you owe me." Claire's voice held a note of desperation, which Aaron mentally zeroed in on. If he could find her weakness, victory would be at hand.

"True," he said neutrally.

"Our parents are not, I repeat *not*, going to get married."

Aaron sat up straighter. "What are you saying?"

"I'm saying that you and I are going to put our devious minds together and come up with a plan to tear them apart."

The girl had clearly gone insane. But as long as he

played along with her, he knew she'd keep talking.

"Now *this* sounds serious," Aaron said.

He could almost hear Claire grit her teeth. "Don't be cute."

"I can't help myself. It just comes naturally." He smiled at himself in the mirror that hung opposite his bed.

"Are you going to help me or not?" Claire hissed.

"Anything for you, Claire." *Anything that will help me worm my way back into your life, as you so eloquently put it,* he added silently.

"Good," she said emphatically. "I'll be in touch."

Aaron opened his mouth to ask her exactly *when* she'd be in touch. But it was too late. Claire had already hung up the phone.

By ten o'clock on Wednesday night, Jake had dialed the first six digits of Louise's phone number exactly fourteen times. He'd kept a running tally in his head each time he'd hung up the phone with his heart pounding.

But he wanted to talk to her. He needed to talk to her. After the meeting the day before, she'd bolted out the door without a word. And that day she hadn't been there at all. Jake missed her, and he still wanted to talk to her about the experience she'd shared.

Jake took a deep breath and punched the final digit. *Fifteen's the charm,* he said to himself as he listened to the phone ring.

"Hi, Louise," Jake said, but her name came out sounding more like "Weez" because he was so nervous.

"Is this Brian? Because if it is, the answer is still no. I never want to see your lying face again."

Jake thought about hanging up. She obviously hadn't

recognized his voice. She could live the rest of her life thinking she'd told Brian whoever to go to hell.

"Hello?" she yelled. "Are you going to say something, or are you just going to breathe heavily, like usual?"

"Uh, it's Jake." His voice was so quiet that he wondered if she could hear him.

"Oh, ah, hi, Jake." She sounded even more embarrassed than he felt. "Sorry about that."

"No problem." He readjusted himself on his bed so that he could prop his head on one elbow.

"What's up?" she asked.

"I was just wondering where you were today. I mean, I haven't talked to you since . . ."

"Since I spilled my guts?" She sounded almost mad that he'd brought it up.

"Yeah." Jake grabbed the plastic cup on his bedside table. Water. He needed water.

"I went to a different meeting today," she said.

He waited for her to say why, but she didn't. "Uh, why?"

"I guess I didn't want to see you."

"Oh." Jake switched the receiver from his left ear to his right. He didn't know what to say. "Why?"

"When I was talking at the meeting, I felt great. Really strong." She paused, and he heard her sigh. "But afterward I felt so exposed. I mean, telling everybody else was fine. They only know me as Louise from AA."

"But?" Jake knew what she meant. It was definitely weird how their relationship—acquaintanceship, actually—had changed through AA. They each had two different lives: one that took place within the confines of that room, and another that took place outside. "But you're in my class. I mean, we've had sex, for God's sake. I just started wondering what you must think about me. Fun Louise, the drunken slut."

Jake squeezed his eyes shut. He had to be honest with her. "I, uh, guess I did sort of see you that way," he admitted. "I didn't really realize it, but even when we went out to dinner the other night, I still thought of you as not all that much more than the girl I had sex with on homecoming night."

Louise sniffled. "Wow, you really know how to pick up a person's spirits."

"But that's totally changed, Louise," he said loudly. "That old image is gone. After your speech, I finally saw the *real* you."

"Really?" She sounded a little better, and he heard her blowing her nose.

"Yes. And the real you is . . . beautiful. Inside and out."

She gave a small laugh. "You don't have to say that, Jake."

"I mean it."

"Well, thanks. I'm, uh, glad you think so."

"So will you come to the usual meeting tomorrow?" he asked.

"Definitely."

"Good night, Louise."

"Sweet dreams, Jake."

Twelve

Aisha was still fuming when she squeezed in between Zoey and Nina onto a bench in the cabin of the *Minnow* on Wednesday morning. On the one day that she'd managed to actually get up when her alarm went off (as opposed to hitting the snooze button four times, the way she normally did), her leisurely breakfast had turned ugly. Before she'd even finished her bowl of cereal, the mere sight of Kalif had made her so mad that she'd stomped out of the kitchen.

By the time she calmed down, she had realized that she would make it to the ferry on time only if she sprinted the whole way. Of course, it was at the exact moment of that realization that she'd spilled half a cup of coffee down the front of her sweater.

"Good morning, Eesh," Zoey said.

"Says who?" Aisha responded, digging in her backpack for her calculus homework.

"I guess we know who *didn't* get visited by the tooth fairy last night," Nina said. "Does the scowl on your face have anything to do with a certain cute nominee for the Westinghouse scholarship?"

Aisha felt her blood pressure rise. "Don't talk to me about David Barnes."

Nina stuck a Lucky Strike between her lips. "Wow,

that guy really gets to you," she said out of one corner of her mouth.

Aisha banged her head against the wall behind the bench. "I'm not too thrilled with Kalif, either."

"What did Kalif do?" Zoey asked.

Aisha put her homework back. She could tell by the direction of the conversation that she wasn't going to accomplish anything before they arrived in Weymouth.

"Ever since David became his math tutor, my brother thinks the Walking Encyclopedia is the greatest thing since Twinkies." She knew she sounded like an immature brat, but she didn't care.

Nina took a long drag on her unlit cigarette. "Ah, yes, the mentor-mentee relationship. It can be quite powerful—sometimes even deadly."

"I don't think *mentee* is a word," Zoey said.

Nina dropped the Lucky Strike and crushed it under the heel of her boot. "The point is, a mentor can be extremely influential. David may brainwash Kalif into sabotaging Aisha's performance on the Westinghouse exam." She wiggled her eyebrows at Aisha. "I'd keep my calculator locked up if I were you."

Aisha groaned. "Nina, your sensitivity is overwhelming."

Nina grinned. "Hey, Claire the ice princess taught me everything I know."

"All I know is that my little brother is delusional."

"What makes you say that?" Zoey asked, sounding concerned.

Ever since she and Lucas had straightened out their latest lover's tiff, Zoey had gone into helping-friend mode. Personally, Aisha preferred her cynical, downtrodden mode. But Zoey had a way of making people talk.

"Last night I was sitting in the den watching David

Letterman. I'd been studying for, like, five hours, and all I wanted to do was relax and listen to the Top Ten list.''

"So what happened?'' Zoey asked.

"Kalif came in and said the most ridiculous thing I've ever heard in my life.'' Aisha felt herself start to blush. Not for the first time, she was glad her dark skin camouflaged the blood rushing to her face.

"Don't keep us in suspense,'' Nina said. She leaned forward and stared at Aisha.

"He said that David Barnes has the hots for me!'' The words rushed out quickly.

"Oh, no! Someone call the lobotomist. An attractive guy has a crush on Aisha,'' Nina shouted.

"Shut up,'' Aisha growled.

Zoey smiled serenely. "You should be happy, Eesh. Maybe you can use your womanly wiles to get David to throw the test.''

"First of all, I fail to see the humor in anything having to do with David Barnes,'' Aisha said. "Second, he does *not* have the hots for me.''

"Maybe *you* have the hots for *him*,'' Zoey suggested.

Aisha didn't bother to respond to *that* statement. The very idea that she found David Barnes the least bit attractive was too ridiculous to contemplate. Really. It was.

Nina knocked lightly on Benjamin's door. So far, her *Cosmo*-inspired plan to make Benjamin jealous hadn't been successful. Between Jake not giving her the time of day and Benjamin not even noticing that Jake wasn't giving her the time of day, she was still exactly where she'd started. But all that was about to change.

"Go away, Zoey,'' Benjamin called from inside. "I'm not in the mood for a pep talk.''

"It's not Zoey." Inside Nina heard Benjamin turn off the symphony he'd been listening to.

A few seconds later he appeared at the door. "You knocked like Zoey."

When Nina had first started spending a lot of time with Benjamin, she'd been amazed that he always knew who was at the door. For a long time she'd thought he had some kind of psychic gift. But eventually he'd explained that every person's knock had its own rhythm.

"I know. I figured that if I knocked like *me*, you'd pretend you weren't home." Although Benjamin had left only a foot of space between himself and the door, Nina managed to squeeze past him. She went straight for the bed.

Benjamin left the door wide open, then moved to his desk chair. "Uh, listen, Nina, I appreciate your stopping by. . . ."

"Do I hear a *but?*" she asked quietly.

"But we don't really have anything to say to each other. It's over." His voice was cold, but Nina detected a slight tremor. Maybe there was still hope.

"Hey, I'm not here to talk about us. That's old news."

"It is?" Benjamin asked suspiciously.

"Yeah." She took a deep breath, preparing herself for the lie she was about to tell. "Anyway, I can't stay long. I'm meeting Jake in a little while."

"Jake McRoyan?" he asked.

"You know, the big, good-looking guy who used to date your sister." Nina smiled. She'd almost convinced herself that she was telling the truth.

"Oh. Well, have fun." Benjamin swiveled in his desk chair so that he was facing his computer keyboard.

Nina's heart sank. He didn't even care that she'd practically just declared her love for another guy. Then again, Benjamin wasn't the type of guy to let his emotions hang out all over the place. Especially lately. Maybe after she left he'd be totally depressed at the thought of her with another guy. Maybe he'd even call her later and tell her he never wanted her to see Jake McRoyan again.

Nina cleared her throat. "So, uh, I guess I won't have time to read to you tonight. Since I'm meeting Jake, I mean."

Benjamin didn't bother to turn around. "Nina, I don't expect you to read to me anymore. It would be pretty awkward under the circumstances."

"Well, somebody's got to do it."

Good going, Nina, she said to herself as soon as the words were out. In Benjamin's current state of mind, she was sure he'd interpret her statement the wrong way. He'd assume that she considered reading to him to be some kind of burden.

"I mean, I want to do it," she added quickly.

Benjamin finally turned around, aiming his Ray-Bans (which he'd had to tape together on one side after his tirade) in her general direction. "I found a replacement," he said.

Nina felt the air rush out of her lungs. "A replacement?" she squeaked. She blinked rapidly, trying to hold back the tears that were welling up in her eyes.

"Lara's going to do it."

Nina was sure she hadn't heard him right. "Lara?"

"Yep." Once again Benjamin turned toward the computer.

"I didn't even know she could read," Nina said. She was so shocked that she momentarily forgot she was heartbroken.

"Ha ha," Benjamin said dryly.

Nina could deal with Benjamin's being depressed.

She could handle his breaking up with her—as long as it was temporary. She could even accept that Lara McAvoy was going to get to spend hours and hours reading to him while Nina was at home alone. But his indifference was just too much to take.

Nina stood up, feeling like a wooden puppet. Her tears were gone, and her eyes were so dry that she felt they might pop out of their sockets. "I guess I'll go now," she said. Her voice sounded strange, as if it belonged to someone else.

With his back to her, Benjamin held up a hand and waved. "Have fun with Jake."

Nina backed out of the bedroom slowly, her eyes focused on Benjamin's rigid spine. At that moment she almost found the strength to hate him.

At five minutes to seven that evening, Lara heard Benjamin's footsteps in the stairwell. She could tell it was him because his cane made a tapping noise every time he climbed another step.

She took one quick sip of Jack Daniel's, then rushed to the small, graying sink that was attached to one wall of her room. She quickly squeezed a blob of toothpaste onto her finger and rubbed it around the inside of her mouth.

She didn't want Benjamin ragging on her about her drinking—she got enough of that from Jake. Not that she was drunk. She'd just wanted to unwind a little before the tutoring session began. But people like Benjamin didn't understand the concept of the cocktail hour.

She spit out the remainder of the toothpaste at the exact moment that Benjamin knocked on the door. She still didn't know why she'd offered to help him. God

...new he hadn't done anything for her. But it was too late to back out now.

Lara took a deep breath and opened the door.

"Hi, Lara," Benjamin said.

"How'd you know it was me?" No matter how many times she encountered Benjamin, Lara couldn't get used to his ability to act like a sighted person. Sometimes she even wondered if the whole blindness thing was an act.

"Does anyone else live here?" Benjamin asked sarcastically.

"Oh. Right." She took a step backward and opened the door wider. "Come on in."

Benjamin walked a few feet into the room, then stopped.

"Don't you want to sit down?" she asked.

Benjamin gave her a half smile. "Sure. If you want to tell me where I can find a chair. Otherwise I'll stand."

"Sorry." She grabbed the wooden desk chair that Christopher Shupe had left behind and stuck it right under Benjamin's butt. "You can sit now."

Benjamin actually laughed. "A simple left, right, or center would have been fine."

"Sorry again." Lara was glad Benjamin couldn't see her blush. She had a knack for saying exactly the wrong thing about his blindness. But it wasn't her fault—she'd never been around a blind person before.

"Nice wallpaper," he commented.

"What?"

"Gotcha."

"Real funny," Lara muttered.

While Benjamin unzipped his backpack and started feeling through it, Lara tiptoed to the shelf where she'd placed the bottle of Jack Daniel's. As quietly as she could, she unscrewed the cap and took a quick swig. Dealing with Benjamin was a two-shot proposition. At least.

"Here's the book," Benjamin announced. He held it out for her to take. "It's *The Metamorphosis*, by Franz Kafka."

Lara replaced the bottle gently on the shelf. "Oh, yeah. That's the one where the guy turns into a huge cockroach and everyone hates him."

"You've read it?" Benjamin asked, looking as if he were about to fall out of the chair.

Lara yanked the book from his hand. "Jeez, Benjamin, I did go to high school."

"Now I'm the one who's sorry."

"Believe it or not, I like books." Not that she'd read any for a while. But Benjamin didn't need to know that.

"I guess I never took you for the bookworm type," he said. Lara was gratified to hear him sounding slightly sheepish. It was nice to be the one in control of the situation for a change.

"I'm an artist. Artists like literature."

"Right. Have you been painting a lot lately?"

Lara flopped onto her bed. Now that the booze was settling in, she was starting to feel more relaxed. "Nah. I've been getting into sculpture."

"Really? Can I see, I mean feel, one of your pieces?"

"Sure." Lara rolled off the bed. Her finished paintings were all stacked up against the wall, but she kept her sculptures on a table she'd picked up when another tenant had moved out of the boarding house. Lara chose a small piece she'd completed the week before and handed it to Benjamin.

He held the sculpture in his left hand, running the fingers of his right lightly over the surface. "This is amazing," he finally said.

"Can you tell what it is?" she asked.

"It feels like some kind of gnome—or maybe a leprechaun." He moved his hand around the sculpture once again. "Am I close?"

"Yeah. It's a banshee." She eyed the bottle on the shelf but decided she'd be pushing her luck to try to snag another sip.

"What's that exactly?" Benjamin asked, handing the piece back to her.

"A kind of fairy. The banshee is the spirit of death." She placed the sculpture carefully back onto the table. It was the best one she'd done so far.

"You know what I'm realizing?" Benjamin asked suddenly.

Lara sat back down on the bed and opened *The Metamorphosis*. "What?"

"You and I really don't know each other very well." He was leaning back in his chair, looking somewhat perplexed.

"That's true," she agreed. "You and your sister haven't exactly been the Welcome Wagon."

Not that she cared. She had better things to do than sing songs around the piano and make chocolate chip cookies, or whatever it was that wholesome, all-American families did.

"So let's start now," Benjamin suggested.

"Why?" Lara asked. What did he want from her?

"I'm feeling totally depressed, verging on suicidal. You seem like a person who could empathize with what I'm going through."

"Oh, yeah. Dark is what I do," she agreed, standing up. If they were actually going to *talk*, she needed one more tiny taste of Jack. "Okay, so let's talk. . . ."

* * *

132

Almost two hours passed before Lara started yawning. She'd worked all day, and the alcohol was making her tired.

"Man, what time is it?" Benjamin asked.

Lara glanced at the travel alarm clock on her bedside table. "A little after nine," she answered, surprised.

She couldn't believe how long she and Benjamin had kept an actual conversation going. What was even wilder was that she'd enjoyed it. Benjamin wasn't the picture-perfect blind wonder boy he seemed. If anything, his problems were even worse than hers.

"I'd better get going." He stood up and stretched his arms above his head, then removed his coat from the back of the chair.

"We didn't even get to the book," Lara said. She picked up the forgotten assignment and placed it in Benjamin's outstretched hand.

"Just tell me what happens," he said.

Lara walked to the door while Benjamin fumbled with his backpack. "He dies from loneliness," she answered, opening the door.

Benjamin grinned. "Don't you just love happy endings?"

"I wouldn't know," Lara said quietly. "I've never had one."

Benjamin reached out and gently squeezed her shoulder. It was a gesture she'd seen him make toward Zoey a hundred times.

"Maybe you'd have better luck if you didn't drown your troubles in whiskey."

Lara gasped. "You knew?"

"When someone reeks of toothpaste, they're usually trying to hide something."

Benjamin gave her shoulder one more squeeze, then

walked into the hallway. As Lara watched him make his way carefully down the stairs, she decided she'd give what he'd said some thought.

But first she needed a drink.

Thirteen

On **Thursday**, Benjamin handed in a short paper on *The Metamorphosis*, in which he discussed the pain of being different in a society that worshiped the mainstream.

After school, Zoey went over to the Geigers' to see how Claire was doing. Claire said she'd be fine as long as everyone quit asking her how she was doing.

Zoey then went downstairs and talked to Nina, who had made the large box that held her Health Rider into a makeshift table. Zoey chose not to comment.

On **Friday**, Nina asked Jake if he wanted to ditch the cafeteria and go to McDonald's for lunch. He said no.

Claire called Aaron to tell him she was ready to hatch a plan. She said he should expect to find her at his dorm sometime Saturday afternoon. After getting directions, she hung up the phone before he had another chance to apologize.

Zoey let Lucas bring Kate over to watch *Sleepless in Seattle*. Afterward Lucas said it was as stupid as it had been the first and second times they'd seen it, but Zoey and Kate both had cried. Zoey decided maybe Kate wasn't so bad after all.

Lara showed up at Jake's bedroom door at two in the morning. She was bombed and tried unsuccessfully to get him to join her in a nightcap. When she finally passed out, Jake lugged her all the way back to her place and put her in bed. On his way home, he decided that he was going to sleep in Wade's old room for a while. He couldn't handle any more late-night visits. In fact, he couldn't handle Lara, period.

On **Saturday**, Claire took the 7:40 A.M. ferry to Weymouth. Twenty minutes after the *Island Breeze* docked, she'd retrieved the Mercedes from the parking garage and was on the highway that would take her to Connecticut.

At noon she stopped at a roadside diner for lunch. Unfortunately, she was so nervous about seeing Aaron that all she could stomach was a cup of black coffee. She told herself, however, that her nerves were due to the zealous nature of her mission to break up her dad and Sarah Mendel. When she went to the cash register to pay for her coffee, a waitress named Michelle informed her that the guy sitting in the back booth had already taken care of the bill. Claire left the diner immediately without looking back. She never did catch the truck driver's name.

Around two-thirty she arrived at the lobby of Aaron's dorm, where he was waiting with a dozen roses. Claire took the bouquet, then dumped it into a nearby trash can.

When they went to a coffee shop to discuss the demise of their parents' relationship, Aaron wouldn't do anything except try to kiss Claire. She left forty-five minutes later, totally disgusted with herself for having made the trip at all.

When she finally got home, she told her dad she'd spent the day at the mall, then caught a movie. He kissed her good night, then repeated for the third time how happy he was that she was going to be one of Sarah's bridesmaids.

On **Sunday**, Aisha woke up to find David Barnes in her kitchen again. This time he was eating French toast and Canadian bacon. She pretended he wasn't there and went straight to the coffeepot. She then retreated to her room until she heard him leave. By the time she got back to the kitchen, her stomach was growling so loudly that her dad asked her if she was having digestive problems.

Nina finally unpacked her new Health Rider and set it up in her room. She used it for fifteen minutes, at which point she collapsed on the floor in a heaving, sweaty mass.

On **Monday**, Zoey ran off a hundred copies of the invitation she'd typed up on Benjamin's computer when he was out. She tried to enlist Aisha and Claire's help in distributing the invitation to the entire senior class. After much discussion, during which Aisha and Claire tried to talk her out of the party altogether, Zoey finally agreed to limit the party to island kids.

Jake told Zoey he didn't want to come to the party if either Lara or a keg was going to be there. She assured him that neither would be anywhere *near* her party, so he accepted the invitation.

*   *   *

On **Tuesday**, Aaron called Claire to tell her he wanted another chance to help her with her efforts to break up their parents. He suggested she come down for the weekend. She told him nice try, but no way. And even if she'd wanted to go, she said, which she didn't, she couldn't because of Benjamin's surprise party Friday night.

Jake asked Louise if she'd like to go with him to Benjamin's surprise party. Louise said she didn't think it was such a hot idea, but thanks all the same.

After school, Zoey, Aisha, and Nina went to the mall. Zoey bought balloons, streamers, and other party decorations. Nina sulked and ate two chili dogs.

On **Wednesday**, in front of Benjamin on the ferry, Nina asked Jake if he wanted to go to the mall after school. He said he had basketball practice, but thanks all the same.

After school, Nina hid behind the bleachers in the gym so she could catch up with Jake after his practice. When practice was over, he took a fifteen-minute shower, then exited the locker room. Nina followed him to the second floor of Weymouth High, where he ducked into a classroom. Thinking she had him cornered, Nina burst into the room, planning to finally clinch her seduction.

Inside the classroom, thirty people were sitting in chairs and drinking coffee. A thirtyish guy asked her what her name was. She replied, "Uh, I'm Nina." Everyone said, "Hi, Nina," right back to her. Except Jake. He just stared.

Nina fled, deciding that her plan had failed.

Surprise Party!

For: Benjamin Passmore's twentieth
           birthday

When: February 28

Time: 8:00 P.M. sharp

Where: Zoey and Benjamin's house

RSVP: Give Zoey your answer, which had
           better be yes, in person.

Fourteen

Claire rang the Passmores' doorbell, then studied the sky. It was filled with low cumulus clouds.

She hadn't been to the Passmores' house since the last time she'd come to talk to Benjamin about his love life. At that time her life philosophy had been pure cotton candy. She'd been so idiotically in love that she'd wanted everyone else to be as happy as she was.

She'd been arrogant enough to think one conversation with Benjamin would snap him out of his depression and get him back to normal. However, she'd vastly underestimated her ex-boyfriend's stubborn streak.

But Claire was sick and tired of watching Nina mope around the house like a puppy who'd lost its master. Claire needed Nina and Benjamin to get back together, if for no other reason than that it would get Nina out of the house once in a while.

Benjamin opened the door and aimed his sunglasses at Claire. "To what do I owe this rare pleasure?" he asked.

"How'd you know it was me?"

"Chanel Number Nine." He stepped back, and Claire followed him into the house.

"Can I get away with saying I was just in the neighborhood?"

Benjamin shook his head. "Don't even try it."

"Okay, then, I wanted to talk to you," Claire said. She moved past Benjamin and headed for his bedroom. She didn't want Zoey hanging around and listening to her every word. She always preferred to do nice things for her sister in private.

Benjamin entered the room behind her and closed the door halfway. "All right, Claire. I'm listening."

She sat down in his desk chair. "I'm worried about you, and Nina's driving me crazy."

Benjamin perched on the edge of his bed and folded his arms across his chest. "I appreciate your concern, but I'm fine. As for Nina, I'm sorry she's getting in your way. But that's really none of my concern."

As Claire studied Benjamin's sardonic smile she felt a flash of nostalgia. With Benjamin, she'd always felt more or less in control. Even when he was reading her mind or making snide comments about some manipulative thing she'd done, he never really broke her cool. Unlike Aaron, who had shattered it—and her. With Benjamin, her relationship had been interesting and manageable. With Aaron, it was interesting and totally out of control.

"Sometimes I wish we'd never broken up." At first she didn't realize that she'd said the words aloud.

"Very funny, Claire."

Claire sat up straighter. "I'm not trying to be funny. I'm serious."

Benjamin stood up and began pacing the room. "I know what you're doing. Zoey and Nina probably put you up to it."

"What in the hell are you talking about?" Claire asked.

"It's the oldest trick in the book," he said, pointing an accusatory finger in her direction. "Build up the blind guy's self-confidence by sending the sexiest girl in school over to his house to tell him she finds him irresistible."

Claire couldn't believe her ears. "Talk about self-absorbed!" she said loudly. "The entire population of Chatham Island doesn't revolve around your funk, Benjamin."

He sat back down. "You mean Zoey and Nina didn't tell you to come over here?"

"No. And I didn't say you were irresistible. I simply said that sometimes I wish we'd never broken up."

"Sometimes I miss you, too," he said quietly.

Claire rolled her eyes. "Now you're the one building false confidence. You're so in love with Nina your brain's turned to sentimental pulp."

"Nina and I broke up," Benjamin reminded her.

"Not because you don't love her." Now she was finally getting to the reason she'd come there in the first place.

"True."

"Why, then?" Claire asked, leaning forward in the chair.

Benjamin shrugged. "Nina seems tough on the outside, but inside she's incredibly vulnerable."

"Tell me something I don't know."

"I don't want her to get so wrapped up with me and my problems that she forgets she has a life of her own. She's so loving that she'd probably give up her own freedom to care for her blind boyfriend. That's not right."

"Don't you think you're being a little melodramatic?" Claire asked. Benjamin was even worse off than she'd thought. If he really meant half of what he'd just said, he was too far gone to be revitalized by a few words from her.

"No, I don't. I also don't think it's any of your business." His voice was flat and resigned, leaving no room for misinterpretation.

Claire stood up. "You win, Benjamin. I'm going to leave you to stew in your own pathetic juices."

Benjamin stood also. "Thanks, Claire. I appreciate that."

"But as your former girlfriend, I feel I have a duty to share a disturbing piece of information with you," she said, walking toward him.

"What's that?"

"Zoey's having a surprise party for you."

Benjamin clutched his head. "Claire, please tell me I didn't hear you right."

"You heard me." Even though she felt sorry for him, Claire was amused by the look of complete irritation on his face. "Zoey would kill me if she knew I told you."

"So, when's the big event?" he asked.

"Uh, Saturday night." She didn't want to totally blow Zoey's big surprise. She just wanted to give the guy fair warning.

"Not Friday?"

"Zoey thought you'd be expecting something on Friday and that this way you'd really be surprised." *Not to mention ticked off at me when you learn the truth*, she added silently.

"Why is she doing this to me?" Benjamin groaned.

Claire shrugged. "She means well."

Benjamin sighed. "The road to hell is paved with good intentions."

"You'll live," Claire said. On impulse, she reached out to give him a kiss on the cheek. But somehow her lips landed on his mouth, and a moment later Benjamin's arms were around her. Suddenly they were kissing. But Claire felt nothing. She closed her eyes and thought of Aaron.

A few seconds later Benjamin broke away. "I don't know why that just happened," he said, sounding confused.

"Old habits die hard," she answered. "But I guess the magic's gone."

Benjamin laughed. "I've always admired your tact, Claire."

"Don't you agree with me?" she asked.

He smiled sadly. "Yeah. It seems you and I are destined to be friends."

Claire put her hand on the doorknob. "There are worse things than being friends," she remarked. *Like being head over heels for the biggest jerk on the planet.*

In the kitchen, Zoey took several deep, steadying breaths. Why had she chosen this particular moment to come downstairs and ask Benjamin if he wanted a snack? If she'd stayed in her room, she'd never have seen . . . what she just saw.

At first she'd thought she was having a flashback. But she'd blinked, and they'd still been there. Kissing. There was no denying it. Claire and Benjamin had been in each other's arms. Lip to lip.

If Nina found out, she'd lose it. She would hate Claire—and maybe Benjamin, too. Nothing on the island would be the same. Zoey put her head in her hands, wondering what she should do.

In a moment the answer came to her. She'd forget the entire incident. As far as she was concerned, she was still upstairs reading *The Metamorphosis*.

Aisha checked her watch and saw that it was 10:05 P.M. Damn. Her physics test was less than twelve hours

144

away, and she still didn't feel totally confident. Oh, sure, any normal person would think that studying her butt off for an entire week would be sufficient preparation. But on their last physics quiz David had beat her by half a point. She didn't intend to let that happen again.

But if she wanted to make the 10:35 ferry, she had to pack up her books and leave the Weymouth library as quickly as she could. *I'll study at home*, she promised herself.

It was the same vow she'd made and then broken every night that week. No matter how good her intentions, she ended up either falling asleep or zoning out on television the minute she got home.

Aisha sighed and began putting her books into her backpack. *This thing must weigh thirty pounds*, she thought. Not only was her brain fried, she'd probably have sore shoulders from lugging around her textbooks.

Aisha sensed his approach even before he said anything. Her nervous system had become so attuned to David Barnes that the hair on the back of her neck stood up every time he came near her.

"Hi, David," she said, her back still to him.

"You knew it was me." He reached her side and leaned against the table. "I'm flattered."

"Don't be. A sudden bout of nausea tipped me off." She finished zipping her backpack and turned to face him.

"You know what I've noticed about you, Aisha?"

"Let's see. Maybe that I can't stand the sight of you?"

David took off his glasses and laid them on the table. Aisha groaned silently. She'd seen him take off his glasses before—the gesture always preceded an insult he was particularly proud of having come up with. "No,

145

that you hide your insecurities behind a smoke screen of false bravado.''

Aisha slammed her fist on the table. It landed just millimeters from David's glasses. ''Want to know what I've noticed about you?'' she asked through clenched teeth.

''Do tell,'' David said, grinning stupidly.

''You're a puffed-up megalomaniac with a slide rule where your soul should be.'' His face was just an inch from hers, and she could see the pupils in his gold-flecked eyes dilating.

''You're kind of cute when you're angry,'' he whispered lazily.

Aisha's blood went from a simmer to a boil. No one, not even Christopher, knew how to punch her buttons as well as David. ''I hate you,'' Aisha shouted.

''Not as much as I hate you,'' David screamed back.

The few people who were still in the library turned to stare, but Aisha ignored them. She kept all her concentration focused on David's mouth, which she was going to punch if he made one more patronizing remark.

''Do you know what else?'' he said slowly, emphasizing each word.

''What?'' she yelled.

''I'm going to kiss you.''

Before the words had fully registered in Aisha's brain, David's arms were around her waist. Aisha started to recoil, but her hands moved automatically to his broad shoulders. As his mouth came closer Aisha felt an electric tingle travel up her spine. Her own lips parted in anticipation of his kiss.

A moment later they were wrapped in each other's arms, kissing passionately. Aisha's brain told her to break away and slap David's face, but her body responded differently. She felt herself melting into his embrace, and it was only the support of his arms, which were surprisingly muscular, that kept her standing.

Aisha's eyes snapped open at the sound of cheers and clapping from the people who'd been staring.

"Nice move, dude!" a guy shouted.

"You go, girl!" yelled Pamela Crisman, who was in Aisha's history class.

David's arms dropped to his sides. He stared at her as if she were a one-celled specimen on a lab slide. "Well . . ."

Aisha grabbed her backpack and started backing away from him. "I—I, uh, guess I'll see you in class tomorrow," she stuttered. Her lips were still tingling, and she wasn't sure she could feel her toes.

"May the best man win on the test tomorrow," David called. His voice sounded high and unnatural, as if he'd just gotten hit in the groin with a soccer ball.

Aisha rolled her eyes, already regretting her moment of psychosis. "I think you mean best *woman*."

As Aisha turned and walked away, she hoped David couldn't tell that her legs were shaking.

Fifteen

"Mom, I'm home," Aisha yelled Friday afternoon.

"How was the test?" Mrs. Gray asked, coming out of the kitchen.

"Not so great." Aisha hadn't been able to concentrate on her physics problems. She'd kept glancing over at David to see if he was looking at her. Of course, he hadn't been.

"Well, there's something on the hall table that's guaranteed to cheer you up," Mrs. Gray said.

Aisha raised her eyebrows and walked to the table. Her heart jumped when she saw the thin white envelope. She knew without looking at the return address that the letter was from Christopher. His handwriting was unmistakable.

Aisha picked up the letter and walked slowly to her room. As she stared at the envelope in her hand, the memory of David's kiss burned a hole from her brain and through her fingers to the paper in her hand.

Christopher's Love Letter

DEAR AISHA,

THANKS FOR THE VALENTINE EVEN IF IT WAS ALMOST A WEEK LATE. I CAN'T EXPRESS HOW MUCH HEARING FROM YOU MEANT TO ME. I KNOW THE POSTCARD I SENT YOU AS SOON AS I ARRIVED WAS RATHER COLD, BUT AT THE TIME I WAS STILL PRETTY SHAKEN UP BY THE STING OF REJECTION (I THINK YOU KNOW WHAT I'm REFERRING TO).

EVEN THOUGH YOU SAID OTHERWISE BEFORE I LEFT, I WAS CONVINCED THAT YOU WERE THROUGH WITH ME. NOW I KNOW THAT'S NOT THE CASE.

BOOT CAMP IS HELLISH BUT FUN IN A PERVERSE KIND OF WAY. I'm ALREADY IN THE BEST SHAPE OF MY LIFE YOU WOULDN'T BELIEVE HOW TIGHT MY QUADS ARE. MOST OF THE GUYS ARE ON THE IMMATURE SIDE, BUT I GET ALONG OKAY WITH MOST OF THEM. (BY THE WAY, WHAT GAVE YOU THE

IDEA THAT I'D EVER SHOW YOUR CARD TO THE
GUYS HERE?)

My COMMANDING OFFICER THINKS I'D MAKE A
GREAT SOLDIER. HE SAYS HE'S NEVER SEEN ANYONE
SO DISCIPLINED. I DIDN'T TELL HIM I'M JUST
IN THE ARMY TO GET A FREE EDUCATION. LET'S
HOPE WORLD WAR III DOESN'T BREAK OUT
BEFORE MY ENLISTMENT IS UP.

BUT ALL OF THIS ARMY TALK IS JUST A WAY
FOR ME TO AVOID THE REAL ISSUE AT HAND: MY
FEELINGS FOR YOU.

I KNOW I WAS A JERK BEFORE I LEFT CHATHAM
ISLAND. I WAS PLAGUED BY THAT MALE EGO
YOU'RE ALWAYS COMPLAINING ABOUT. BUT I DO
LOVE, YOU, AISHA.

WHEN I'M LYING AWAKE IN MY BUNK AT NIGHT,
I DREAM ABOUT THE MOMENT WHEN WE'LL MEET
AGAIN. I CAN ALMOST SEE YOU STANDING ON THE
DOCK AS MY FERRY COMES INTO THE PORT.
BELIEVE ME, I WON'T WASTE ANY TIME RUNNING
DOWN THE GANGPLANK AND SWEEPING YOU INTO MY
ARMS.

I'D BETTER GO NOW. THEY'RE PLAYING TAPS,
WHICH MEANS LIGHTS OUT, NO EXCEPTIONS. BE
GOOD, AND WRITE ME SOON.

LOVE,
CHRISTOPHER

P.S. SAY HI TO EVERYONE FOR ME.

P.P.S. TELL THAT DAVID BARNES JOKER THAT HE'D BETTER BE NICE TO YOU—OTHERWISE HE MIGHT FIND A FIST IN HIS FACE.

Sixteen

By seven-thirty on Friday night, Nina had paced back and forth across the living room enough times to leave a permanent track in the rug.

"I shouldn't be here," she said for the tenth time.

"Don't be ridiculous," Zoey responded, also for the tenth time. She was standing on a small stepladder, holding one end of a Happy Birthday banner.

"Benjamin hates me," Nina moaned.

"How does this look?" Zoey asked. She hopped off the ladder and moved back to view the sign.

"Who cares? Benjamin won't be able to see it anyway."

"I care," Zoey said.

Nina sank onto the couch and observed the living room. Zoey had strung streamers across the doorway to the kitchen, and there were balloons of various colors lying everywhere. "I shouldn't be here," Nina repeated.

Aisha emerged from the kitchen. "You're the one who agreed with Zoey that this stupid party was a good idea," she snapped.

Nina whistled. "Forget to take your happy pill today?"

Aisha set the bowl of Doritos she was carrying onto

the coffee table. "You're not the only one who has problems, Nina."

"If you two don't stop bickering and start getting into the party spirit, I'm going to make you bob for apples in a vat of salsa," Zoey said. "So shut up and have a good time."

Nina grabbed one of the noisemakers that Zoey had put on the sofa and gave it a loud blow. "Hey, these are almost as good as cigarettes," she commented.

"Maybe you can kick the habit," Zoey said. She folded the stepladder and headed toward the kitchen.

"I don't know how you two can joke around at a time like this," Aisha blurted.

"A time like what?" Zoey asked. She didn't look pleased that Aisha was continuing to spoil the aura of forced festivity that had permeated the house all afternoon.

"Poor Christopher is locked up in some bunker," Aisha said.

Zoey put down the ladder. "First of all, Christopher is at boot camp, not in a bunker. And he's there by his own volition. Furthermore, I fail to see what that has to do with my trying to do something nice for Benjamin."

"Forget it." Aisha stuffed a handful of Doritos in her mouth and hung her head.

"Come on, Eesh. Even a self-centered pitymonger like me can see that something's wrong with you," Nina said. She hadn't seen Aisha look so tortured since she'd been debating about whether or not to marry Christopher.

Aisha wiped the Doritos crumbs from the sides of her mouth. "I, uh, I guess I just miss Christopher," she said.

Zoey sighed. "That's too bad, Eesh. But try not to be a buzz kill, okay?"

Aisha produced an artificially wide smile, which made her look more like a pit bull than an attractive woman. "From here on out, it's party, party, party," she said.

Nina blew the noisemaker again. This surprise party was starting to feel like the Last Supper.

"Here, Benjamin, try this," Darla Passmore said, putting yet another plate down in front of him.

He sighed. "Mom, I've already tried four new kinds of pie. I'm full."

What had started out as a simple taste test at Passmores' had turned into a marathon of eating. His mom was trying to develop a new menu, and she'd decided that Benjamin should be her guinea pig. He'd already eaten parts of six different meals.

"This one's special," she said. "It's birthday cake."

"I don't feel much like celebrating," Benjamin said heavily.

He'd been dreading the surprise party that was going to take place on Saturday night ever since Claire had taken pity on him and told him about it. He'd spent most of the day trying to think of a way to evade the event. Somewhere between southwestern meat loaf and Yankee bean soup, he'd come up with a plan. First thing in the morning, he was going to beg Lara to guide him to a movie theater in Weymouth and leave him there until the 10:40 P.M. ferry. She was the one person who'd have no problem hurting Zoey's feelings.

Benjamin heard his dad sit down in the chair across the table. "Benjamin, you're twenty years old today. It's a time for happiness. You've got a lot to be thankful for."

Benjamin felt like barfing. He was sick of everyone telling him to have a positive attitude. He didn't have crap to be thankful for. He was a twenty-year-old blind guy who'd probably be dependent on his parents for the rest of his life.

"Thanks for the song and dance, Dad," he said. "But you really have no idea what I'm going through." He pushed back his chair and grabbed his cane.

"Benjamin, wait!" Mrs. Passmore called.

"I'm sorry, Mom, but I've got to get the hell out of here. I just want to be left alone."

"Let him go, Darla," he heard his dad say as he walked out the door.

Outside, Benjamin breathed deeply. More and more, his life felt like a prison. He walked slowly up Dock Street, savoring the moments before he got home. He was sure Zoey would be bouncing around the house trying to act as though everything were peachy keen. She'd probably even have some kind of fake birthday celebration to keep him from guessing that she'd planned a party.

As he turned up South Street, Benjamin's mind drifted to the kiss he'd shared with Claire. She'd been right that any sparks they'd once shared were gone. When they'd kissed, he'd closed his eyes and pretended she was Nina.

Benjamin finally reached the path that led to the Passmores' front door and made a sharp right. At least he hadn't gotten lost again—that was one good thing he could say for his twentieth birthday.

Nearing the house, he noticed an eerie silence. It was almost as if the people who lived there had packed up and gone away. Well, he was glad there was quiet. Maybe Zoey was at Lucas's, and he could avoid her altogether.

Benjamin opened the door and headed for his room, thinking of which CD he wanted to play first. Something by Ray Charles, he decided as he walked through the living room.

"Surprise!" a chorus of voices suddenly screamed. Benjamin jumped. "What the—"

"Happy birthday!" Zoey shouted, hugging him.

"Uh, thanks." He was going to kill Claire.

"Happy birthday, Benjamin," he heard Nina say quietly. A moment later her lips brushed against his cheek.

"Thanks, Nina," he said, hoping his voice didn't betray the fact that the touch of her lips had sent shivers running through him.

Benjamin stood rooted to the spot while Jake, Lucas, Kate, and Aisha each took their turn greeting him. He tried to smile and seem enthusiastic, but he secretly wished the floor would open up and swallow him whole. This scene was exactly what he *didn't* need.

Finally Claire approached. "Surprised?"

Benjamin grabbed her arm. "You said the party was tomorrow night," he hissed.

Claire pulled her arm gently from his grasp. "Come on, Benjamin, I couldn't spoil *all* the fun. Zoey never would have forgiven me."

Benjamin shook his head. Leave it to Claire to have the last laugh.

"Having fun?" Zoey asked cheerfully.

"Where's Lara?" he asked, aiming his broken Ray-Bans at the spot where he thought her face was. With so many voices surrounding him, it was difficult to get his bearings.

"Lara? Why would she be here?" Zoey asked.

"Because she's our sister," he said quietly.

"Excuse me. I didn't know you two were so close." Zoey sounded hurt, and Benjamin felt a wave of guilt. She'd tried to do something nice, and all he felt was hostile and ungrateful.

"Sorry, Zo. Never mind."

Zoey put her arm around his shoulder. "It's forgotten," she said. "Now smile. I have a feeling tonight's going to be one of the best nights of your life."

Or the worst, Benjamin countered silently.

Aaron

In all candor, I must admit I'm one of those lucky people who doesn't have much need for revenge fantasies. The trick is never to let anyone get the best of you. As long as you situate yourself so that you're in charge of every situation, life usually works out in your favor.

That having been said, I wouldn't mind seeing Lucas Cabral caught in one of his dad's lobster traps. Not because I feel the need for revenge against him. I just plain don't like the guy.

Seventeen

Aaron whistled to himself as he headed up South Street. He had every reason to feel good. His performance at Gray House, where his mom had been staying since Thanksgiving, had been worthy of an Academy Award. She'd totally believed him when he'd said he had wanted to surprise her with a visit.

He'd even managed to get her to talk him into going to the party at the Passmores' rather than have dinner with her and Burke. Aaron smiled to himself. He had a feeling that his reconciliation with Claire was mere minutes away. When she realized he was devoted enough to haul his butt all the way to Chatham Island for her, she'd have to forgive and forget. No woman could resist such a romantic gesture.

When he arrived at the Passmores' front door, he decided against knocking. If Zoey answered the door, there was a distinct possibility that she'd slam it in his face. Starting the evening on that kind of note would be ill-advised.

Aaron walked into the house and headed for the living room. REM was blasting from Zoey's boom box, and judging from the noise, the party seemed to be in full swing.

He saw Claire immediately. She was lounging on the

couch, wearing tight black pants and a sheer black silk blouse. The sight of her made him catch his breath.

He leaned against the wall just inside the living room door, waiting to be noticed. It didn't take long.

"Aaron!" Zoey shouted. "What are you doing here?"

The room became instantly quiet. Someone turned off the music. "I wanted to wish Benjamin a happy birthday," he said. *Among other things.*

Claire didn't say anything. She just stood up and walked swiftly toward the kitchen. Aaron started to follow, but a soft hand touched his shoulder. He turned around and saw that Kate had approached from behind.

"Hi, Aaron," she said quietly. "Thanks for the 'day after' call."

Aaron raised one eyebrow. "I have no idea what you're talking about."

Kate's face fell. "Look, I'm not going to stand between you and Claire. But don't pretend you don't remember what happened the other night."

"When are you going to get the picture, Kate?" he said. "I'm not interested. And I never have been."

"That's enough, Mendel," Lucas said. He'd come up to Aaron's side without him noticing.

"As usual, you're sticking your nose where it doesn't belong, Cabral," Aaron said smoothly.

"I'm not the one who's crashing the party," Lucas replied.

Zoey moved in between them. "Guys, I'm trying to have a nice, friendly party here. Why don't you let it go for one night?"

Aaron smiled at her, making sure to flash his perfect white teeth. "Great idea, Zo."

He recognized a chance for escape and got away from Lucas Cabral as fast as he could. Leaving Zoey to stroke her boyfriend's ego, and Kate to stand there looking stupid, he made a beeline for the kitchen.

Claire was at the sink, washing dishes. "Go away," she said without turning around.

"Claire, we need to talk."

"No, we don't." She set a glass on the drying rack and reached for a plate.

Aaron crossed the room in two long strides and tried to slip his arms around her waist. She sidestepped him. "Don't even think about touching me."

"I love you," he said, reaching for her one more time.

"You love yourself." Claire started walking toward the living room.

She was just playing hard to get. He was sure that if he persisted, she'd finally melt into his arms. He followed her into the other room, by that point not caring who heard their conversation.

She was already on the other side of the room, standing by herself next to the television set. "I'm not going to leave you alone until you forgive me," he yelled.

"Then you'd better make sure the Passmores don't mind a permanent house guest," she called back.

"Claire, please . . ." He stood still, wondering what the best course of action was. He'd never had so much trouble with a girl, and he wasn't sure how to proceed.

Out of the corner of his eye, he saw Kate coming toward him. *Great*. "Aaron, maybe you should just go," she said.

"Maybe you should find someone else to harass," he responded loudly.

Once Claire saw that he didn't give a damn about Kate, she'd come to her senses. She'd realize Kate meant nothing to him, while Claire herself meant everything. This was perfect.

"Sorry," Kate said. A tear slipped down her cheek.

Claire finally started walking over to him. *Aha!* he thought. His brilliant mind had finally come up with the winning formula. But Claire didn't look very loving when she got near enough for him to read her expression.

"Apologize to Kate," Claire ordered.

This was not going as he'd planned. Not at all. "What?" he asked stupidly. Everyone's attention was now focused on him.

"I think you heard her," Lucas shouted. He let go of Zoey's hand and walked slowly toward Aaron.

"You again," Aaron said when he got close.

"Apologize," Lucas said, his voice trembling with fury.

"You can forget the macho act, Cabral. Everyone knows you're a wimp."

"You're going to regret you said that," Lucas shouted.

"Make me," Aaron challenged.

Lucas lunged forward with his fists out. Aaron jumped backward into the kitchen as Kate rushed in front of Lucas to stop him.

But she was too late. Lucas's left fist hit Kate squarely in the nose, while the other made contact with the middle of her forehead. Kate collapsed onto the floor.

Jake had been sitting in the recliner next to the sofa, watching the entire scene unfold. He'd spent most of the party talking to Aisha, who kept making weird comments about love and betrayal. He'd spent the rest of the party avoiding Nina, who'd been freaking him out for the last two weeks. Luckily for him, she seemed to have been avoiding him as well.

He'd been in the middle of thinking about Louise Kronenberger's breasts when he saw Lucas lunge. Snapping out of his daydream, Jake bolted from the chair and sprinted across the room.

Since Lucas and Aaron were still screaming at each other, he was the first to actually kneel at Kate's side. Her face was pale against her soft red hair, and her breathing seemed shallow.

"Kate, are you okay?" Jake asked, shaking her gently.

There was no response.

"Oh, my God," Zoey said. She'd knelt down on the other side of Kate's inert body.

"Is she all right?" Claire asked, approaching.

"No," Jake said. Blood was pouring from her nose, and her forehead was red where Lucas's fist had landed. "She's unconscious."

Finally Lucas and Aaron stopped shouting. "I hope you're happy," Zoey yelled at them.

"Calm down, Zoey," Aaron said.

"You shut up," Claire snapped.

Lucas crouched at Kate's feet. "I'm so sorry." He looked stricken. "I'm so sorry."

"I'm sure it wasn't your fault, Lucas," Benjamin said. "Whatever it was, exactly."

"Hey, it's not a party until something's broken," Nina said. No one laughed.

Jake shook Kate again, but her head just flopped lifelessly from side to side.

"Someone call an ambulance," Claire shouted.

Aisha ran toward the kitchen. "I'll do it."

Jake stared at Kate's face in horror. The blood from her nose seemed to be coming out faster—a stain had already spread across the front of her white T-shirt. Jake untucked his own plaid flannel shirt and quickly tore a strip from the bottom. Then he folded the cloth and pressed it firmly against Kate's nose. "I think we'd better get her some air," he announced.

Jake picked Kate up and cradled her easily in his arms. Her head was pressed against his chest, and a steady stream of blood continued to flow from her nose to his shirt.

"They're on their way," Aisha yelled. "But it's going to take them a while to get here all the way from Weymouth."

"We'll have to do whatever we can," Jake answered, still walking toward the front door. In his arms, Kate felt like a delicate doll.

Everyone followed him into the front hall, the argument between Lucas and Aaron momentarily forgotten. "Open the door," Jake said.

Zoey cracked the door open, and a blast of cold winter air blew into the house. Jake laid Kate carefully on the floor, then continued to shake her shoulders gently.

The sound of everyone's voices faded to a dull roar behind him as Jake concentrated on bringing Kate back into the land of the living. "Come on, Kate," he whispered. "You can do it."

Still there was no response. In desperation, Jake leaned forward and opened the door wider. As he leaned back to try yet again to revive Kate, he saw a beautifully wrapped package sitting on the doorstep. A piece of white paper was taped to the side of the gift. *To Benjamin, from Lara*, it read.

Jake's heart stopped. Lara had been there. That night. He pushed the thought out of his mind. Just then he had to worry about Kate Levin, not Lara McAvoy.

"Is she any better?" Aisha asked anxiously.

He shook his head. "I don't know."

Jake put two fingers against the pulse at Kate's neck.

Her heart seemed to be beating more strongly, and a small bit of color had come back to her face. "Wake up, Kate," he urged.

A moment later her eyes fluttered open. "Where am I?" she murmured.

At the sound of her voice, Lucas, Claire, and Zoey rushed forward, pushing Jake out of the way. "You're back!" Lucas said happily.

"I just had a great dream . . . ," she whispered.

Jake stood up and looked at the present on the door-step again. Just the sight of Lara's name caused a cold chill to run through his already freezing body. If he saw that girl again in this lifetime, it would be too soon.

Something made Jake move his eyes from the package to the bushes next to the house. He gulped. In her denim jacket and tight faded jeans, Lara was crouching close to the ground.

Jake didn't wait for Lara to realize that he'd seen her. No one noticed as he slipped quickly into the house and past the group knotted around Kate. On his way through the living room, Jake picked up his ski jacket, then bolted toward the Passmores' back door.

As he sprinted through the cold, dark night, Jake thought of Kate's smooth, pale face. "I'm glad you're okay," he whispered softly into the wind.

Making Out:
Who Loves Kate?

Book 15 in the explosive series about broken hearts, secrets, friendship, and of course, love.

Nina's lost **Ben**, **Aisha's** split with **Christopher**, and **Claire** hates **Kate** because she kissed **Aaron**. But **Kate** is dreaming of the mystery guy who saved her at **Ben's** party. Will she ever discover...

Who loves Kate?

Love stories just a little more perfect than real life...

Don't miss any in the

enchanted♥HEARTS
series:

Calling all tEEN Readers:

Do you like to read great books
featuring characters you can relate to?

Do you have strong opinions and lots of ideas
about books and reading?

Want to get free books, sneak previews,
and other stuff?

Send for a FREE sampler of some of the greatest
Teen fiction being published now and find out how you
can join the Avon Tempest Forecast program!

Avon Tempest is a brand new publishing program especially for
teen readers, featuring characters and situations you can relate
to. Return the coupon below, and for your trouble we'll send
you a sampler featuring excerpts from four great brand new
Avon Tempest books, including <u>Smack</u> by Melvin Burgess, <u>Little
Jordan</u> by Marly Youmans, <u>Another Kind of Monday</u> by William
Coles and <u>Fade Far Away</u> by Frances Lantz—plus information
on how you can join the Avon Tempest Forecast program to get
news of what's new at Avon Tempest and more free reading,
plus a chance to give us your ideas and feedback about what we're
doing.